TRACY WEIMAN
ÁINE MᶜWRYAT

Larp.

RED ADMIRAL PRESS
amsterdam

Red Admiral Press

Text ©2009 Tracy Weiman
Illustrations ©2017 Áine McWryat

Amsterdam, the Netherlands

9 8 7 6 5 4 3 2 1

978-90-826624-3-6
9082662434

for R. N.
the inventor of Larp

One

"Now, what's it going to be then, eh?"

The man who spoke these words leaned back in his office chair and placed the tips of his fingers delicately together.

"Hmm? What what what . . ."

He sighed and gazed off into the distance with a dreamy sort of look.

"There are so many things I would like to do to punish you," he said, "so many. But almost all of them are illegal nowadays. Boiling you in oil, locking you in cupboards, placing you in the stocks, that sort of thing. Pity."

In the room with the man were two girls, sitting in two little chairs opposite his vast oak desk, and they watched him silently with wide eyes.

"And so, my dears, once again I pose the question — what shall it be this time?"

"How about," suggested the girl in the right-hand chair, "slightly restricted cafeteria access?"

"In this school, that would fall more into the *reward*, rather than the *punishment*, category, I think," said the Principal. "Any other ideas leap to mind?"

"You could always," said the girl in the left-hand chair, "expel us . . ."

"EXPEL YOU?" roared the Principal, suddenly jumping to his feet. "And leave you two FREE, each and every day, ALL day, to wreak more and more HAVOC upon the helpless and unsuspecting citizens of Snudsley? NEVER!"

With a strangled cough, he finally regained control of himself, and wiped his forehead with a handkerchief as he began to pace stiffly around the room.

"No," he said thoughtfully, "oh no, I'm afraid a simple expulsion won't do. I have a responsibility. What's been going on in this school is all too fantastic. Let's refresh our memories, shall we?"

"Actually, I think we remember perfectly —" began the girl in the right-hand chair.

"Last year," continued the Principal, picking up a sheet of paper from his desk and reading it, "your newspaper announced that the Biology Department was sponsoring a *Giraffe Dissection Workshop*, and hundreds of eager students showed up with scalpels, only to be informed that no such animal was in residence. In your defense, you claimed that 'giraffe' was a misprint for 'tiny frog'."

The girls grinned a little bit.

"Six months ago," the Principal went on, "you reported on a new Australian sport called 'Galumpty', which was apparently a sort of ping-pong played with very old eggs. Mr. Collar in the Gym tells me that the resulting craze among the students could hardly have been smellier."

The girls grinned a bit wider.

"You announced a 'Model-For-A-Day' program in the Art Department, and advised all the children to come nude to class. You claimed that the Italian teacher was actually a robot being secretly tested by the Italian government — to prove it, you suggested that the students try to hit him with little hammers and listen for the *ping*."

The left-hand chair girl giggled, and then tried to turn it into a throat-clearing noise. The Principal wiped his brow again, and swallowed very hard, as if he was trying to get his stomach to accept something that it was quite sure it didn't want.

"And finally, if these weren't enough lies," he continued in a cracking voice, "one week ago, you claimed that I — myself, Keith Willoughby Box, Principal of the Snudsley Middle School — am actually an escaped convict," (he

consulted the paper again) "'armed and dangerous', it says, and that I am at this moment on the run from the police!"

"And . . . ?" asked the girl in the left-hand chair.

"Oh — and also that my real name is Fingers McGee!"

"Actually, Mr. Box," said the girl in the right-hand chair, "it was *Knuckles* McGee, and . . ."

"Whatever it was!" shouted the Principal, flinging the paper away. His mustache was so stiff and prickly now that it looked as though it might jump off his upper lip and dash around the room, like a squirrel.

"But really, sir," said the girl in the left-hand chair, "we haven't actually done anything, we just put funny made-up things in the paper. They weren't really lies, not exactly. We didn't think anyone would take them seriously."

"Ah yes, *The Snudsley Suggester*," said the Principal, trying to regain his professional calm and seating himself slowly at his desk. "You've hit the nail on the head. I have decided that therein shall your punishment lie."

"How do you mean, sir?" asked the girl in the right-hand chair.

"The newspaper," smiled the Principal. "It's over. It's defunct. It's out of business. Washed up and wiped down."

"But . . ."

"Wait — I'm not done yet," said Mr. Box. "It's Gettysburg. It's history. It's gone gone gone. Wave goodbye because there it goes. Off into the sunset. As of this afternoon, when people refer to your paper, if they refer to it at all, it will be as *The Snudsley Ex-Suggester*."

And with that he stood up, smiled broadly, and rubbed his hands gleefully together. Rennie Parsley and Velly Sprout looked at one another glumly, and then pushed themselves up out of the little chairs, their shoulders slumped and their heads hanging low.

"Now — go!" said the Principal, opening his office door. "And don't be so gloomy. I'm only shutting down your paper, not sending you off to prison — drat the luck!"

The two girls sighed, shuffled through the door silently, and the Principal slammed it triumphantly behind them.

By George, that served them right, he thought. *Clever girls, to be sure, decent families, clean and tidy — but then why couldn't they stop with all this nonsense? What gets into them? Why couldn't they stop causing mischief and go back to studying about President Van Buren and French Verbs and Magnesium Nitrate, like good little children?*

"It was different when I was a boy," he said aloud, strolling over to the window and smoothing out his mustache. "No nonsense then — no funny business. Sensible. Everything on the up and up."

He looked out the window behind his desk and onto the playground below. Strange, it seemed there were two pigs there. Two large black and pink pigs. No students at all. Unusual.

No pigs in the playground in my day, he thought.

Now there were three pigs. Now six, and now sixteen. And they had been joined by a number of goats as well. And he thought he could see a sheep or two.

As he watched, the entire playground became completely overrun by a massive amount of pigs, sheep and goats, with a fair sprinkling of farmers thrown into the mix.

Principal Box looked upon the tinkling, bleating, oinking and grunting scene, frozen stiff with rage. His eyes bulged out and his mouth fell open, so that he looked like one of those big fancy goldfish you see floating around in the aquarium at the dentist's office.

"Whaaaaa —?" he wondered aloud.

"Howdy, partner!" shouted one of the farmers from below. "Y'ain't gat any carrots for my little goat Sheldon here, do ya?"

"Sheldon?" whispered Principal Box.

"Or turnips mebbee. He's mad for turnips!"

Mr. Box's eyes slowly grew wider and wider, and his face grew redder and redder. He opened his mouth to speak, but no sound came out, only little puffs of steam. Finally he took a deep breath, and —

"SPROUT!" he cried. "PARSLEY!"

The two girls walked silently back to the empty classroom that served, when school was over for the day, as their newspaper office. Renate Parsley was the taller of the two, with reddish-blonde hair and blue eyes, and a sort of lurking smile on her lips that never quite went away, no matter how she happened to be feeling.

Velvet Sprout was a bit shorter and plumper, and had a much darker complexion — curly brown hair and brown eyes that looked perpetually a bit fretty. I don't know if 'fretty' is an actual word, but that's how they looked.

"Do you suppose," said Velly, settling into a chair, "we ought to have told the Principal about the 'Snudsley Pig-

and-Goat Beauty Contest' posters we put up all over town last week?"

"What difference does it make?" said Rennie. "It's too late now. It looks" (she sniffed the air) "actually it *smells* as though its already started."

"Oh boy, that Box is a rotten egg," said Velly angrily. "Imagine shutting down the paper just because we made up a few stories. Maybe we should start a new paper, but print what actually happens."

"But *nothing* happens!" said Rennie in exasperation. "That was the whole point. We *had* to make up our own stories because nothing ever happens."

"I know, I know" said Velly. "It's sad. And this week's edition would have been our masterpiece."

She picked up a sheet of paper from the table and read the story out loud —

EXPERTS PROPOSE
HUGELY ENORMOUS STRING MUSEUM
FOR SNUDSLEY

In an effort to raise the cultural tone of the Snudsley area, the Town Council have this week approved a plan to build a massive, modern complex of buildings to house the string collection of Snudsley's famous founding father, General Cuthbert Snudsley, who famously lived in the 19ᵗʰ century and also famously collected string.

"This will be a place where people from all over the United States, and indeed from all over the world," stated one expert, "can come and look at some really really important strings."

Plans for the museum, which is expected to cost 500 million billion dollars, include a grand "Hall of Threads", an interactive "Strings Alive!" exhibit for children, and a sweeping "Twine Wing". An authentic Renaissance-style theatre will regularly perform classics like Shakespeare's Stringio & Threaderick *and Fletcher's* King Edward the First: or, The Piece of String.

"It will be a true Wonderland of Strings," continued the expert, "a place where anyone can come and spend the whole day exploring the fascinating history of everything in the whole entire world and also some string."

"It would have been *The Suggester*'s biggest scoop," said Velly, "if it had really happened."

"Well, it's too bad," said Rennie, "but cheer up, Vel. *The Suggester* may be kaput, but who's to say our fun is over? We have an enormous new task ahead of us: *revenge*. We can dedicate the rest of our lives to getting back at Box."

Velly had to agree, but of the two of them, she was always more inclined to look on the bleaker side of things. Besides, she had been the *Suggester*'s Head Writer, and Rennie had been the Chief Editor. She liked writing the funny stories.

She heaved another deep sigh, picked up another newspaper and read it out loud —

PEANUT BUTTER "COMPLETE NONSENSE", SAY EXPERTS

Experts declared today at an informal meeting of the World-Wide Peanut Use Advisory Board (WWPUAB) that the phrase "Peanut Butter" was misleading, inaccurate, and just, to be honest, stupid.

"The Americans and British call it peanut 'butter', the Dutch call it peanut 'cheese', and it's neither of those," said one expert in a highish sort of voice. "The Germans are perhaps the most accurate in calling it a 'cream', though it's actually a sort of icky purée. And the Argentinians simply pretend that it doesn't exist. It's time for a Comprehensive Pan-Continental Peanut Butter Control Policy (CPCPBCP) that everyone can live with."

The proposed name for the smeary, faintly nauseating food-type substance would be "Larp" — a name decided upon after 3 years of inter-departmental debate, several referendums in different countries, and at a cost of over 400 thousand jillion million dollars. The altered labels will be required by next week.

Rennie sat down next to her friend, and patted her gently on the back.

"If completely stupid and pointless made-up lies could be poetry," she said kindly, "that's poetry."

"Thank you," sniffed Velly.

Now at this same exact moment, Principal Box had just finished ejecting all the pigs, goats, sheep, and farmers from the school property, and it had taken some doing. Thoroughly annoyed, he stood in the middle of the playground, in what remained (and you can perhaps imagine what remained) of the Snudsley Pig-and-Goat Beauty Contest.

He was angry, and he was tired. He felt a faint buzzing in his head. He hadn't ever felt it before, and he didn't understand it — and Keith Box was someone who felt very uncomfortable when he didn't understand something.

As he made his slippery and stinking way back to his office, the buzzing became louder and louder, and began to shape itself into a single word in his mind:

By the time he had cleaned off his shoes and reached his office chair, the doubts were gone and he was sure that the expulsion of Renate Parsley and Velvet Sprout from the Snudsley Middle School was far from being the last thing he wanted to do. It was actually the one thing in the world he most wanted to do.

Brilliant! he thought. *They will leave school, become criminals, and end up in jail. And I can help!*

There would be problems, of course. He knew it. It's hard to expel anyone without any real crimes, and the Principal only had the made-up stories they had put in the newspaper. He would have to be clever — the PTA would be sure to pour buckets of trouble down upon him were he to punish Rennie and Velly without an iron-clad case against them.

No, what he needed was to arrange for one of the girls to turn on the other and rat her out, and then sign an accusation against her friend. That would be solid evidence.

"And one of them will crack, I'm sure," he nodded to himself (if you actually can nod to yourself), "and then, after the first one has finked, I can get the other one so mad that she will sign too, and accuse the first one. Hee hee! When I have two signed accusations I will be able to toss the both of them out into the street in half a second, PTA or no PTA!"

Quickly, and with a sinister smile, he grabbed his

appointment book and flipped it open to the following day's page.

"Wednesday, 9:00 sharp," he giggled as he wrote, "that Parsley girl!"

❖ ❖ ❖ ❖ ❖

Abigail Braintree was a little girl who lived down the road from Velly's house, and she was four and three-quarters years old, as she would be happy to tell you, over and over and over, if you ever met her. She had two — I suppose you *could* call them "dolls" — that she carried with her constantly. One was called "Soapy" and had once been a dog of some kind, but now looked like a legless, eyeless, and furless sausage. The other was a plastic female torso with one arm. It had been a Barbie doll in the distant past, and this one's name, for some reason known only to Abigail herself, was "Rumba".

RUMBA   SOAPY

Abigail was hard on her toys but even harder on the grown-up boys and girls around her, for she was never happy with kids her own age and always wanted to be with the older children. This fascination wasn't mutual; all the older kids usually ran away screaming when they saw her little form toddling down the sidewalk towards them.

When Abigail wasn't wondering about why all the older kids didn't want her hanging around with them, she was trying to hang around with them. And she had a specially robust fixation on Rennie and Velly, accompanying them everywhere they went. She would be waiting to follow them to school in the morning, wait around on the school grounds for them all day, and then follow them home again in the afternoon. Somehow — Rennie and Velly never saw how exactly — she managed to get back to her own home every evening, only to be at their front doors again the following morning.

And whenever she was with them, she pummeled them with her fascinating conversation:

"I'm four and three-quarters years old. We saw a dolphin last summer. I like pudding. Mommy's going to make Rumba new eyes. Where are you going? Can I go? We saw three dolphins last summer. I'm four and three-quarters years old."

As anyone can tell you who knows a four and three-quarters year old person, this sort of thing can go on for hours and hours. Rennie and Velly had learned that they couldn't get rid of Abigail, but also that it was fairly easy to ignore her as she tagged, forever babbling, at their heels.

She had come to school with them the next morning, and had watched the entrance door close behind the two girls with a tear in her eye, because that closing door meant she would have to spend the day alone in the playground, grinding Soapy and Rumba into the gravel around the swing-set and gurgling. So imagine her delight when, five minutes later, Rennie came back out the door and started to walk across the playground towards the Principal's office. She was off like a dog after a stick.

"Hi Rennie. Hi Rennie. Where're you going? Can I come? I gave Soapy a bath and now he smells. We had cabbage and apple sauce and toothpicks for dinner. Cabbage is a vegetable. Then we had to go to bed. What did you have? For dinner I mean? What did you have? Where're you going?"

"Abigail!" said Rennie sternly. "I just found out that I have to go in to the Principal's office right now, so I'm going there."

"Why?"

"Because I have to."

"Why?"

"I don't know!" said Rennie. "Stop asking me! Because I'm in trouble, I guess!"

Abigail turned pink, and looked shamefacedly down at her shoes.

"Why?" she asked.

"Just wait out here and be quiet," said Rennie. "Look, here's a rhododendron bush under Mr. Box's window. Just stay under here and pretend you're a snail or something until I come back. A *quiet* snail."

Abigail immediately threw herself down into the dirt under the rhododendron bush and began wriggling around, saying "Shh" and "Quiet" to herself. Rennie rolled her eyes and pushed open the door to the Principal's office.

Principal Box rose from his seat, smiling, and extended

a hand to Rennie as she walked into his office.

"Lovely to see you, young lady," he beamed. "I'm so glad you could find time for me in your busy schedule."

Rennie looked around, but there wasn't anyone else in the room.

"Please *do* take a seat, Miss Parsley," he said, motioning her towards the large plush armchair that had taken the place of the little wooden stools. Rennie inched over to it cautiously and sunk in.

"Now . . . Miss Parsley . . . nice day, isn't it?"

Miss Parsley? Had he gone utterly bonkers? Where was the cherry-colored ball of rage with a mustache that had been in his office yesterday?

"Comfortable?" he crooned.

"Um, I guess so," said Rennie.

"Now I'm awfully sorry that I had to *pretend* to be so angry yesterday," he said, flicking out his mustache ends and sliding around the side of his desk. "Had no choice with the Sprout person in the room, you see?"

"You mean Velly?"

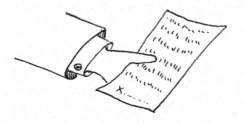

"Of course, Velvet Sprout," he continued. "You both ran that newspaper and you both are due for punishment — the rules are rules, and I'm terribly sorry, but there's nothing I can do about it."

"Okay," said Rennie.

"Of course, I know *perfectly well* that it was the Sprout who actually wrote all those ridiculous stories, wasn't it?"

"Well, yes, it was," admitted Rennie.

"You see? She alone is guilty. So, if you would, sign this paper stating that the whole thing was all her fault, and then the outcome for you might be more — *pleasant*," he grinned, and pushed the paper towards her.

Rennie wasn't particularly afraid of Mr. Box, and she certainly wasn't worried about being punished — she had been too deeply in trouble too many times for that. But this was a new twist.

"I'm sure a clever girl like you can see that it's really quite a *reasonable* thing to do . . ." he oozed.

But all she could think to say, as Mr. Box grinned at her over the sheet of paper, was —

"Are you *nuts?*"

"*Nuts?*" repeated the Principal, straightening up and turning slightly pink again. Rennie noticed the mustache getting bristly, right on cue. "*NUTS?*"

"Yes, that's right, nuts. Cracked! Certifiably insane! Out of your tree!" laughed Rennie. "You're saying — I'm not responsible? Velly did everything? And I'm going to admit it? Oh *please!*"

Rennie knew that she shouldn't laugh at the Principal, and that he could make lots of trouble for her. But she couldn't help it — he was staring at her and looking exactly like a teakettle that someone had welded shut to see how long it would take to explode. He got red-der and redder, and she tried harder and harder to bite her lip and choke the laughter down, but it didn't work — it just came out louder.

Of course, it was no surprise to Principal Box that he wasn't well beloved by the students,

but still, he wasn't used to them calling him a perfect idiot and laughing merrily in his face. And he didn't take it well.

"Here! Now! You little —" he shouted. "Sign it, now!"

"But I don't have a pen!" giggled Rennie, pushing the paper back at him.

"Very well, Parsley" said Mr. Box threateningly, "if you won't sign this paper, then I can't be responsible for the consequences. And you will live to rue them, yes I said RUE THEM!"

He snatched up the unsigned paper and stormed out of the room, slamming the door behind him. A moment later he returned.

"What am I doing? This is my office — get out, Parsley!"

"Okay," said Rennie, gasping for breath. She got to her feet and went to the door, turned and spoke very calmly.

"If you are trying so hard to get me to squeal on Velly, you must not have enough evidence against us to do anything worse than shutting down the newspaper. Right?"

The Principal glared at her.

"And now that you *have* shut it down," she continued, "and you can't get rid of us, Velly and I will just have to go and amuse ourselves in some other way, won't we. I wonder what *that* will be like. Don't you?"

Mr. Box felt a cold chill go down his spine as he watched her walk, smiling sweetly, through the open door.

It was already mid-morning recess when Rennie left the administration building and came out into the bright sun of the schoolyard. She saw that Velly was sitting under the Snudsley Oak, reading a book, and that Abigail had left the rhododendron bush and was sitting next to her, pressing Soapy and Rumba into the ground.

She marched up to them without a sound, glared at the two of them for a moment, and then threw herself, like a sack of beans, down into the grass.

"What's wrong, Rennie?" asked Velly.

"Nothing," snapped Rennie. "Why do you ask that? Why should you think something's wrong?"

"Because you're fuming," said Velly, putting her book aside. "You're not only fuming, but seething. And when you fume and seethe together that usually means that something is wrong."

"It's Box!" said Rennie. "I'm so mad at that man I could explode and sew myself up again and then fill myself with explosives and then explode again."

"Pretty angry," said Velly.

"Box! Fume! Seed!" cried Abigail to nobody, and she started to bash Rumba's head into a large knot-hole in the trunk of the Snudsley Oak. (Oh, I suppose that I should explain what the Snudsley Oak was. It was a very big and old oak tree that grew in the middle of the schoolyard, and it was supposed to have been planted by the town's founder, General Cuthbert Snudsley.

I say "planted", but the actual story is a bit different. As we already know, he collected string as a hobby, and in those days he would keep all his strings in wooden chests,

made of oak wood — and supposedly he forgot about one of these chests and left it outside in the rain for so long that it sprouted and became a oak tree. Completely stupid, I know, but that's the legend.

Anyway the Snudsley Oak was very famous throughout the Snudsley region, which I suppose says something about the Snudsley region.)

"Plus I'm so wholly and thoroughly *bored* with this place," Rennie continued. "Now that we don't have *The Suggester* anymore to spice things up, life seems pale and wan."

"I know what you mean," said Velly. "I've become so bored I'm reading *The Secret Garden*."

"Good heavens," said Rennie, "imagine being as bored as that!"

She sighed heavily, lay on her back, and looked up at the sky. It certainly was a beautiful late spring morning, and, as Rennie gazed upwards through the gently waving branches of the Snudsley Oak, she could see a slow-moving train of dappled silver-grey clouds floating majestically across the azure expanse, now and then peeping between the lush green leaves, and she heard the tiny little birds singing their songs, and she felt the dew-fresh breeze blow across her face like a promise of the full-flowering summer that was coming — a summer abounding in the scents of honeysuckle and melon and roses and all rich, ripe, fine, good things.

"*BOR-ING*!" said Rennie, and she sat up again. "Really boring. You know what, Velly?"

"What?"

"I've been thinking about peanut butter."

"You have?" said Velly. "Imagine being as bored as *that*."

"No, I mean the story you wrote in *The Suggester*, about Larp," said Rennie. "You know, as a story, I never was too fond of it."

"You weren't?"

"I don't know," continued Rennie, "the more I think of it, I guess it just didn't speak to me. It didn't have any *oomph*, it didn't have any *zing*. It just sat there — I mean as a made-up news story it just wasn't ridiculous enough."

"What?" began Velly.

"Now, don't be all hurt," said Rennie. "As a story, you know, it wasn't silly enough. But as an *idea*, it's genius."

"Okay . . ." said Velly slowly, and wondering what on earth Rennie was talking about.

"So Velly," said Rennie at last, "what if, what if, what if — we really did it?"

"What if we really did *what*?" said Velly

"Listen," continued Rennie excitedly, "Boxy won't allow us to publish your story about the peanut butter, right? There's nothing we can do about that. The plug has been pulled. So — why don't we just start doing it?"

"What, you mean start calling peanut butter 'Larp'?"

"Not just *calling* it 'Larp'," said Rennie. "Your story called for the jars to be re-labeled, so we'll re-label the jars — every one of them. We'll print the labels ourselves and

stick them on. And we'll go from town to town, from street to street, plastering every jar of p.b. we can find with Larp labels."

"Every peanut butter jar, all over the country?" asked Velly. "We couldn't!"

"Well, no," said Rennie. "We couldn't do *every* jar.

That would be impossible. But we could do enough so that people will notice. We could start a trend. And if we could do enough jars, the story might even get into the real paper. Imagine."

At these words Velly got a far-away look in her eye. She *could* imagine — her stupid peanut butter story reported as actual news in the *Snudsley Evening Star* or in *The Snudslian*. That would be just too exciting!

"But what if we get caught?" she asked at last.

"We *will* get caught," said Rennie, "that is precisely the point. We're sure to get caught, sooner or later. But it is such a pointless thing to do, no one will even realize what is happening until we have already done hundreds of peanut butter jars."

"I get it," said Velly excitedly, "and when the store manager or someone finally does catch us, we will simply tell the police and the mayor and anyone who will listen that the only reason we did something so senseless was because Mr. Box shut down our harmless after-school paper. He drove us into a life of crime! It will be all his fault!"

"And it will be true, too," said Rennie. "He'll be in so much trouble with the PTA, he'll have to wear a disguise and leave the country if he ever wants to work again!"

"Brilliant!"

"Exactly!"

The bell rang, and both Rennie and Velly picked up

their belongings and started towards the classrooms — but not Abigail, who stayed where she was, having a grunting conversation with Soapy and Rumba on the grass.

"What exactly did the Principal say to you in there?" asked Velly.

"I'll have to tell you later," said Rennie, "I'm going to be late to class."

"I was there!" said Abigail proudly. "I was a snail in a romdondron bush!"

"Listen," said Rennie quickly, "meet me here after school, under the tree, and we can start planning out *Operation Larp*. There's a lot to do."

"I'll be here," said Velly, and Rennie dashed off.

Velly had intended to dash off too, but she didn't, because she suddenly noticed that Abigail wasn't making Soapy and Rumba talk in nonsense sounds; they were talking in reasonably clear English.

"Velly did everything! I'm not ponsible! I will sign a paper!" said the little girl in her high-pitched Soapy voice, and then Rumba said in a growly voice —

"Sign it!"

And then in a high-pitched voice —

"Don't have a pen! Hahahaha!"

"Abigail," said Velly, "what are you talking about? Where did you hear that?"

"Rennie said 'Velly did everything'," explained Abigail.

"Rumba heard Rennie say it this morning, under the window. I was in a bush. She signed it."

"She did? Where?"

"At the mustache-man's," said Abigail, and went back to her imaginary conversation.

"Mitt it Rennie! Grrrb! Have a pen!"

Velly put *The Secret Garden* under her arm and walked off in a daze. It couldn't be, there had to be some other explanation, there had to be. Rennie wouldn't blame her, she just wouldn't do that. They had always been best friends. Abigail must have heard wrong. There had to be another answer, a logical answer, because Velly and Rennie were *very best friends.*

Or at least Velly thought they were — until she got to her own classroom and Mrs. Wheeny informed her that now *she* was wanted in the Principal's office.

Immediately.

Two

"Stupid newspaper. Strings, of all things, peanut butter nonsense. Should never have started. Big mistake, in trouble now. Italian robots, giraffes, strings. Peanut butter nonsense —"

This is Velly, muttering to herself as she walked along to the Principal's office, lost in a tornado of confused thought. She often talked to herself when she was nervous and in trouble — and she was nervous now. She had been called to the office; that always meant that she was in big big trouble.

The only thing for Velly to do was to worry and fret and mumble "peanut butter, good grief," and "string museum, of all the ideas," over and over.

"Where're you going Velly?" said a voice, from somewhere under her left elbow. Abigail was having a very good day — she usually didn't get to see either Rennie or Velly at all until the school day was over, and now they had each been called out of class separately and sent to the Principal's office.

"Abigail," explained Velly, "I'm in a hurry. I don't have time to chat right now, I have to go to the Principal's —"

Abigail opened her mouth.

"— and no, you can't come along."

Abigail closed her mouth again.

Velvet hurried on and entered the administration building. At the end of the hall she saw the dark, heavy door with the word "PRINCIPAL" painted on it in gold letters. She dreaded what waited for her on the other side of that door. She couldn't even bear to turn the doorknob; she just stood outside and felt her stomach turn inside out.

"Miss Sprout?" said a jovial voice from behind the door. "Is that you? By all means do come in."

She did — expecting to be whomped with a big hammer or something the second that she opened the door. Instead she found the Principal gesturing to a large armchair with a big smile.

"Won't you be seated?"

Like Rennie, Velvet looked around to see the person standing behind her to whom the Principal was speaking. But no, there was no one there. He meant her.

She slid into the armchair, and stared at him, and gulped down the dryness in her throat.

"Comfortable?" asked Mr. Box.

Velly nodded.

"I suppose," said Mr. Box, "that you have heard that I had your little friend Parsley in here this morning?"

"Um, yes."

"And so, you no doubt know that she implicated you, Miss Sprout, as the sole instigator of the terrible bundle of falsehoods, fibs, fabrications and fairy-tales that was *The Snudsley Suggester*."

"Well, I . . ."

"Oh, it's *true*," he lied. He sat down again at his desk and placed his fingertips together — his favorite pose. "I have her *signed statement* of that fact. Well, actually I don't have it any longer, it's in the hands of the police at the present moment. But I assure you that it does exist."

Velly didn't know what to think — but she was now sure that Rennie had, in fact, betrayed her. The *police*. It was terrible.

But "Um," was all she could think of to say.

"Now, be assured, I'd like to help you, Miss Sprout," continued the Principal. "I like you. Always have. I even suspect that this *signed accusation* against you is untrue —"

"It *is* untrue," whispered Velly.

"So," said Mr. Box, pulling out a sheet of paper from a

drawer in his desk, "if you will sign this statement, which says that the newspaper was all the work of that Parsley girl, I might be able to persuade the police chief *not* to sweep you out of bed at midnight and plonk you into prison."

There are times when things look so bad, so indescribably bad and awful, that it seems like the only thing that you can keep about you is your self-respect, and you feel as though you can endure anything as long as you have the knowledge that you are honest about *something*, even if it's only one little thing.

True, it generally happens only when you are quite certain that you are about to be arrested and put into a prison cell, but it does happen. And it was exactly how Velly felt right now.

"I *could* sign it," she said at last.

"SPLENDID!" squealed the Principal. "Here's a pen — do you have enough ink — is there —"

"But I won't," continued Velly. "Sorry, sir, that was a comma. I don't care what you do to me, but we did everything in *The Suggester* together, and I won't sign anything that says any different. Ever."

I don't think it's really necessary to go into any detail about the Principal's reaction to Velly's words as they began to sink in — red face, googly eyes, prickly mustache, hair on end, steam out of ears, etc.

"Now, if that is all sir," Velly smiled weakly, "I'd like to go home and pack some things for my trip to jail, if that's okay."

After school, Rennie sat beneath the Snudsley Oak at the appointed time, full of ideas about *Operation Larp*.

She knew it would be necessary to find a brand of peanut butter with an easily removable label, so that the phony labels could be substituted easily and quickly in the supermarket. And they must have a brand whose graphic style they would be able to copy easily with the computer — the idea being that only the words "peanut butter" would be replaced with the word "Larp", and everything else on the label would stay the same.

That would be tricky and would require some research. It was important that the labels should look as authentic as possible, just as though the company itself had changed the name from "peanut butter" to "Larp".

It was already 3:30, and Velly was late.

"I wonder where she could be," Rennie wondered.

"She wanted to go to the mustache-man's," said Abigail.

(Abigail was there too, but you had probably already guessed that.)

"To the Principal's? Why?" asked Rennie.

"She wanted to go fast — she had something to talk about. Something portant. I couldn't come."

That's odd, thought Rennie. What on Earth could Velvet want to see the Principal about? Maybe she was pleading with him to let her start up the paper again — she really loved writing for *The Suggester*. But why wouldn't she talk to Rennie first?

"Listen, Abigail," began Rennie, but she didn't finish because she suddenly felt the presence of someone standing behind her back. Rennie turned, and saw Velly standing above her and glaring down angrily.

"Oh hi, Vel," said Rennie. "Listen, I've been jotting down some ideas for this whole Larp thing, and —"

"Well, don't let me stop you," said Velly, "jot away and keep jotting. And while you're at it, you can jot down that I want nothing to do with *you*, or with *Larp*, or with *anything* having to do with you or Larp for the rest of my life, Renate Parsley!"

And she stormed off, without another word.

To say that Rennie was flabbergasted would be an insult to all flabbergasted things.

"What the heck?" she wondered.

"She's all upset," said Abigail. "She was all upset when she went to the mustache-man's to talk to him."

"To talk to him about what?" asked Rennie.

"Urm," said Abigail, sticking out her tongue and trying to remember. Finally she said —

"Oh, I member now. It was 'peanut butter nonsense'."

So Rennie didn't sleep — not because of worrying about the trouble she might be in, but because she thought Velly had blabbed to Principal Box about Larp. She was so angry and hurt that she didn't even want to see Velly's face, or hear her voice.

But she had to go to school, and would have to walk past the Snudsley Oak, where she and Velly would always meet before the first bell, so that they could go in to class together.

Except she won't be there today, thought Rennie, *not after ratting me out like that.*

But to Rennie's great surprise, as she rounded the corner and headed towards the school entrance, Velly was in her usual spot, holding her books and leaning against the trunk of the massive tree.

"Just like nothing happened," said Rennie to herself angrily.

She knew suddenly what she would do — she would walk right by Velly without a word, without even a glance in her direction. Velly would call out to her, and cry out, and beg her to stop, but Rennie would sweep past her as if they were total strangers. That would show her!

And so Rennie clenched her fists and marched with

furious steps down the sidewalk, in through the gate and past Velly and the Snudsley Oak. She was marching with such determination that she had already reached the front door and turned the knob before she realized that Velly hadn't cried out, or run after her, or noticed her at all.

"What on earth . . ?" thought Rennie.

With equal determination she marched straight back to the Snudsley Oak, ready to give Velly a piece of her mind after all. But when she got there she saw that Velly wasn't ignoring her — actually, she was fast asleep.

"GOOD MORNING!" screamed Rennie into her friend's ear, when she was close enough, and Velly jumped three feet in the air.

"HOW'S THE LITTLE TRAITOR TODAY?"

"Traitor?" mumbled Velly, yawning. "Traitor? That's nice coming from a 24-carat fink like you, Parsley!"

"Didn't you sleep well, dear?" said Rennie with a scowl. "Conscience bothering you? Too many cozy chats over tea and cookies with the Principal, I'll bet."

"No I didn't sleep well, since you ask," answered Velly, "in fact I slept extremely badly. I guess that comes from expecting to be dragged from my bed by the police at any moment during the night — thanks to that accusation against me you signed yesterday, you quisling!"

"I didn't sign anything," said Rennie, "and anyway, what about you, blabbing to the Principal about our Larp slash peanut butter plans? It was such a great idea, and you had to go and tell Box all about it!"

Velly looked confused.

"Wait — you — you didn't sign anything?" she asked.

"Of course not!" said Rennie indignantly. "The creepy old twerp tried to get me to sign some stupid piece of stupid paper saying *The Snudsley Suggester* was all your fault, and I just laughed at him. Laughed! In his face!"

"Uhh . . ."

"And then you pay me back by running off at the first moment and ratting out our Larp idea to him. I could . . ."

"But I didn't say anything about it," protested Velly, "he tried the same trick on me!"

"What?"

"He called me in to get me to sign the same paper against you."

Rennie and Velly each took deep breaths, and they looked at each other.

"He did?" asked Rennie at last.

"Yes," said Velly, "and I didn't sign it either. And trust me, he doesn't know about Larp. I never mentioned Larp and neither did he."

"But when he told you that I signed the paper, why would you believe him?" Rennie snapped. "You know I wouldn't have ever done that!"

"I *didn't* believe him, but I heard it from Abigail," said Velly. "And where did you ever get the idea that I had spilled the beans about Larp?"

"I heard — it from —"

Slowly they both looked down at Abigail, who gazed up at them with a graceful smile. She waggled Soapy and Rumba happily.

"Gfrsszx!" she said.

"One thing is certain," said Rennie. "We've got to keep Abigail Braintree out of this. I don't know how to do it, but we have to try."

Now that they knew for certain that they hadn't betrayed one another, Rennie and Velly were again the best of friends, and even more resolved to get even with the Principal for trying such a sneaky trick. It was full speed ahead with *Operation Larp*, and they had a lot of work to do, so that very afternoon found the two girls sitting at the dining table in Velly's house.

"I know," agreed Velly. "All Abigail did was listen, get confused, and open her fat little mouth. Result: the Principal almost expelled us, plus we were only a step away from a murdering each other. If she knew anything about Larp — anything at all — my gosh! Not only would we get caught, but we probably wouldn't get out of prison again until we were sixty-three."

"So what can we do to get rid of her?"

"Well," said Velly, "I would love to tie something like eight hundred helium balloons to her and watch her gently drift away — but it isn't practical, and it isn't legal."

"Still," said Rennie thoughtfully, "the idea has its own peculiar charm . . ."

"Of course she knows where we live, and she follows us everywhere, but I think we *can* manage to keep her out of our actual houses. We just have to make sure we do all our Larp preparations inside, and never out."

"Good," said Rennie. "Too bad about the balloons, though."

"Now, here's what I've worked out so far," said Velly, as she pulled out a sheaf of notepaper. "First, I think we need a fairly common brand of peanut butter with a very simple label, something all the stores carry."

"Right."

"Second, it should be a jar with only one label in the front; not two labels, front and back. Less work for us."

"What's a quisling?" asked Rennie.

"What?"

"What's a quisling? You called me a 'quisling' earlier. What is that, anyway?"

"It's an old-fashioned word for a traitor," said Velly. "I always wanted to call somebody one, but I never had the opportunity. I thought it might be fun for once."

"And was it?" asked Rennie. "Fun, I mean?"

"Not really, no," said Velly. "Now, the third thing is the most very important thing, Rennie, so listen carefully. We have to —"

But Velly never finished about the very important third thing, because at that moment Mrs. Henderson burst in, jumped up onto the table, and began to squawk and howl, and flap, and hop up and down, and throw feathers around, and I just realized that I completely forgot to tell you who Mrs. Henderson was.

❖   ❖   ❖   ❖   ❖

There are three kinds of people in the world: those who like ducks, those who don't like ducks, and those who don't really have an opinion about ducks.

If you like ducks, please read on.

If you don't have an opinion about ducks, you should also read on.

If you positively don't like ducks, you can skip to page 75, but I wouldn't recommend it, because there are other things in this next part as well. If you like, you can read the parts about Rennie and Velly and their families and just *blip* over the duck parts if they make you uncomfortable.

To start with, Velvet Sprout lived with her parents, Ken and Lily Sprout, at number 3 Grout Lane, Snudsley. It was a comfortable old brick house, nestled between number 11 and number 15, and the reason number 3 came between 11 and 15 is that her house used to be number 13 Grout Lane, but the 1 fell off at some point and no one could ever find it again.

Before Velly was born, Ken and Lily had banged out all the inside walls of their house, so that now it was just a very large single room with all sorts of different "areas"; a kitchen area, a television area, bedroom areas and so on.

They thought it would make the house seem roomier, and that they would have more space. This may sound a bit peculiar but it worked very well. I'll bet you never thought how much space in your house is used up by walls and doors, and the spaces behind the doors where they need to swing out, and the stairs, and the spaces under the stairs, and all of that. Well, Ken and Lily wanted lots of space, and they didn't like having to open and close a hundred doors every time they needed to get somewhere, so their house became a big empty space inside the four outside walls, and Velly thought it was the nicest home in the world.

But the Sprouts hadn't stopped at converting their house into a sort of cozy barn, they also decided to change their back yard into an vegetable garden. They were Idealists, and had lots of notions about how people could live better lives if they stopped paying other people to do things for them and did them on their own. For Ken and Lily, the first victim of this Ideal Life was the vegetable section of the supermarket. They got fed up with the fact that all the vegetables came wrapped up in plastic, like dry cleaning, and decided to grow their own vegetables. So they pulled out the lawn, the barbecue, the stone path and the flower beds and planted lots of vegetables, with the usual cucumbers, carrots, tomatoes and so on — but soon they also had quite a few useful animals about the place.

Ken and Lily were *collecting* people, and when they had one thing, they thought it would be twice as nice to have two of that thing — and that applied to chickens, ducks, pigs, and goats as well. At one point Ken was so crazy for home livestock that he thought he would like to raise trout in a corner of the garden, and he got so far as to dig out a fish pond and fill it with water, but he had to abandon the scheme because the goats kept falling into it.

"Could be a goat pond?" he said hopefully.

"There's no such thing as a goat pond," said Lily.

In their younger days Ken and Lily — in common with lots of other people at that time — like to express their Ideals by marching around and carrying painted signs if they didn't agree with something somebody else was doing. In fact, it was during one such episode, when their local grocer decided to stop stocking healthy whole-wheat bread and start selling pre-packaged, sliced white bread, that Ken got an idea for a home business that would change the life of the Sprout family.

"Lils," said Ken (Ken always called Velly's mother "Lils"), "Lils, I've got it!" He was carrying a sign that said UP WHEAT, DOWN WHITE!

"What's that hon?" asked Lily, who was carrying a sign that had FLOUR POWER printed on it.

"A muffin company," breathed Ken, with a distant look in his eye. "An all-organic muffin company. We'll make a fortune!"

And as Ken and Lily now had to run their very own business by themselves, they soon discovered that they didn't have time for all their animals, and it usually fell to little Velly to feed, look after, and clean all of them — and she became rather good at it. That was something to be proud of; it was quite a thing to be a kind of zookeeper when you're only seven years old. But as she grew up, and needed to spend more time for school, the Sprouts found that they had to get rid of most of their animals because nobody in the family could give them the care they needed. Luckily the animals were so tame and friendly they could sell them all off to different petting zoos.

But since Ken and Lily were collecting people, every time they sold off a duck or a goat, they would add another little decorative *thing* to their collection. There were an astonishing number of these little things hanging around — things that the Sprouts had collected over the years and that weren't of very much value, except that Ken and Lily liked them. A toy walrus hung on the wall next to a chestnut pan. A shoehorn hung under the stairs, over an elaborate lace doily. A pinecone hung under a model car, which hung

VELLY'S HOUSE

next to a picture of Gandhi in a brass frame, over which was suspended a stuffed gecko. All the tables and bureaus were covered with thousands of little objects too — tiny rockets and antique hat stands and silk fans and souvenir teacups. In this sense, the extra space in the Sprout home came in very handy, and the enormous single room never felt too big or too empty. And though Velly missed having her animals around, she also spent lots of happy hours as she grew older, discovering the many treasures nestled in all the endless nooks and crannies.

Ken and Lily ran their organic muffin company out of their kitchen area, and they sold their creations to all the health food shops and supermarkets and restaurants in the town. Every evening you could find Lily, a slim little woman with long red hair and gold spectacles, busy in the kitchen, making tray upon tray of Cauliflower Marvels or Celery Delights. Meanwhile Ken — Velly's father, who was a box-shaped sort of man with curly blond hair piled up on his head, and who always wore a kind and slightly confused expression on his face — would load up their old Ford van for tomorrow's deliveries.

Their muffin company, which was called *The Muffin Company*, had done fairly well in the past, but I'm sorry to say that it wasn't making very much money at the time of this story. The tastes of the muffin-buying public wax and wane, and just now the public wasn't terribly interested in muffins that tasted exactly like cabbages.

Nonetheless Ken was always trying to come up with new ideas to make the business more successful. He once tried to stick little apple leaves into the tops of the apple muffins, to make them look less like muffins and more like apples. They didn't. But then again, they were more successful than his Pine Cone Cookies, his Forest Floor Fritters, and his Bird Nest Biscuits.

These failures never seemed to dim his enthusiasm, though, and Velly would often find herself in dinner table conversations like this one —

"Listen, Lils," said Ken one evening, "listen. I think it's a crime that people are putting butter and sometimes even *jam* all over our beautiful, natural, healthful muffins. It's a crime is what it is."

"Sometimes they use margarine . . ." suggested Velly.

"Yipes!" squeaked Ken. "Margarine is even worse!"

"Well," said Lily, "there isn't that much choice, is there? It's butter or margarine or jelly or nothing at all."

"Lils," gasped Ken, half rising slowly out of his chair, "you're a *genius*." His eyes were fixed on a distant point on the horizon, and he started to grin vacantly. If you had seen him, you might have thought he was having a fit. But Lily and Velly had seen it time and time again. It was a Big Idea.

"Uh, oh," murmured Lily.

"Lils," said Ken again, "you're exactly right. That's the answer. It's new. It's brilliant. It's genius. It might even be," he lowered his voice to a whisper, "profitable."

"What might be?" asked Velly and Lily together.

"*Veg-Spreads*," he breathed. "That's what we'll provide — an organic and healthful alternative to fatty and flavorful butter."

"Hmm," said Lily doubtfully. "Just what do you mean, dear?"

"Gourmet vegetable spreads," said Ken, his eyes shining with joy. "*Veg-Spreads*, made exclusively by *The Muffin Company*. Cucumber Marmalade! Bean Butter! Kale jelly! Lettuce Chutney! It's a winner!"

Velly looked over at her mother, who looked back at her. They both felt a bit queasy at the thought of Bean Butter, but Ken didn't notice. He dropped his fork and stumbled out into the garden like a man possessed.

"Oh goodness," said Lily quietly, as she watched her

husband disappear out the door. "We'd better prepare ourselves, my dear."

"Prepare for what?" asked Velly.

"I love your father," said Lily sadly, "but if one of these Big Ideas of his doesn't catch on soon, I'm afraid we won't be able to stay in Grout Lane any longer. This big house is too expensive. We'll have to sell the place and move to someplace cheaper."

"Move? Out of our . . ."

Velly looked at her mother, and then slowly around her at her warm and cluttered and well-loved house. It impossible to imagine that some other people might move into her house, might put up walls and doors, or even worse — might take down all the lovely things from the walls, and throw them away. And where would they live?

"Oh mom, it won't come to that, will it?" she asked. "One of dad's ideas *could* work, couldn't it?"

"Well, maybe —" said Lily with a sad little smile.

"Eggplant Crème!" said Ken, coming back in from the back yard, his arms laden with bulby purple vegetables and his face shining with joy.

"Eggplant Crème! La crème du eggplant! We're rich I

tell you, filthy rich!"

He ran back out, and a few of the eggplants fell from his arms and bounced over the floor.

"— and then again," continued Lily, "maybe *not*."

If Velvet Sprout had been born a graceful gazelle, and Renate Parsley had been born a small tub of lemon-flavored ice cream, their lives couldn't have been more different. For one thing, while the Sprouts lived in their cozy, cluttered house on one end of Snudsley, Rennie and her family lived in a gloriously modern chrome and glass living space on the other side of the town.

The little village of Snudsley was once called Snudsley-on-the-Drip, a long time ago.The Drip was the river that ran through the whole town, and the Parsleys had the good fortune to have it running through the bottom of their back yard. They were so proud of this fact that they put a small, brushed aluminum plate over their front door with the name of their home engraved on it — DRIP MEADOWS.

Like the Sprouts, the Parsleys also worked from their home, for both Clive and Helen Parsley were not only Rennie's parents but also a business firm: *Parsley & Parsley, Architects.* They had designed and built the home themselves, before Rennie was born, and it reflected both their tastes

perfectly. They liked things to be simple — so simple, in fact, that you couldn't understand them.

For example, if you went to Rennie's house and wanted to wash your hands in the bathroom sink, you probably wouldn't know how to do it, because both the faucet and the knob that turns on the water would be two little chrome balls that looked exactly the same, one on top of the other. After fiddling with them for half an hour you might be able to get the water on, but then how could you figure out the hot and cold? And anyway, where were the towels?

Clive and Helen had designed the kitchen to have cupboard doors that were smooth metal plates set into the wall, and then painted precisely the same color as the wall itself. The result? It was impossible to tell where the cupboards actually were unless you stayed there and looked for them for at least a week, and no one ever stayed there for a week, because there was a good chance that if you did you would starve to death.

Now, although the firm of *Parsley & Parsley* were a

RENNIE'S HOUSE

highly professional and efficient team, Helen and Clive Parsley as parents were perfectly warm and lovable people, though perhaps a bit odd. For one thing, they liked to dress exactly alike, in black trousers and turtleneck sweaters, and they both wore similar round eyeglasses framed in heavy black plastic. They were even of similar heights, so that if Clive hadn't been as bald as an egg you might not be able to tell them apart.

Whereas Velvet Sprout had grown up surrounded by antique coffee cans and tame rabbits and goats, Renate Parsley grew up surrounded by books — lots of them. In fact, if you could have seen the bookshelves that lined practically every room of her home, you might have said "all of them". Like the Sprouts, the Parsleys were also passionate about collecting, but in their case they were perfectly mad for books of every kind — mostly lavish design books like *1001 Woolen Socks* and *1001 Tiny Folding Pocket Rulers*, and *The Toothbrush: from 906 to the Present* — but also books about other architects, books about movies, books of plays and poems, lots of novels and stories, and lots of books about artists with all sorts of lovely pictures in them. And of course they had plenty of storybooks and picture books for Rennie.

Just as most parents do for their children, Clive and Helen used to take turns reading Rennie's storybooks to her before she learned to read them for herself. But unlike most children, Rennie could never have a special story that she would want to hear over and over again in the same way, and that was because Clive and Helen would always get bored with the stories and change them each time they read them.

Perhaps the first time that Little Red Riding Hood came to Grandmother's Cottage, the wolf would be in bed waiting for her. But the next time it might not be a wolf, but a stick insect. And the next time it might be David Attenborough, or the Gulf of Mexico, or a box of chalk. And it was that way for every single one of Rennie's storybooks.

"So Jack climbed up the beanstalk, up — up — up —" Helen would say in dramatic voice, "and when he reached the top, what do you think he saw?"

"The giant's castle?" little Rennie would say with wide eyes.

"Nope, Denver International Airport!" exclaimed Helen. "And he bought a ticket to Milan, and he opened a combination gas station and car wash, and he lived happily ever after."

Rennie grew to like that way of telling stories very much, and it made her terribly curious about what would happen to Jack or Rapunzel or Red Riding Hood the next time she got to hear the story. Sometimes she would even try to imagine the endings, but she never got it right.

"And the prince approached the castle," Clive would read, "and the bramble grove magically parted for him, and allowed him to enter through the front gate. And there, in the central chamber, still golden and glorious and everything after a hundred years, there was a beautiful bed. And in the bed there lay —"

"A plate of boiled eggs?" suggested Rennie.

"Sorry, no," said Clive, closing the book and shaking her head, "and you were so close, too."

"Oh . . ."

"No, daughter, I'm afraid it was all the members of Abba. And they lived happily ever after."

Telling stories in this way to a young child is almost certainly going to give that child an incredible imagination and a restless sense of humor, and Rennie was certainly loaded with those. Over the years she developed a talent

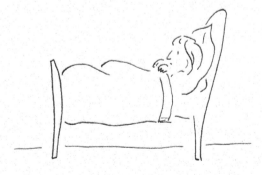

for seeing common and everyday things in unusual ways, and for thinking up absurd and screwy practical jokes. She was quite proud of the fact that she never could have gotten into so much trouble with things like *The Snudsley Suggester* if she hadn't been so creative and imaginative — two qualities she inherited from her peculiar parents.

However, even though Clive and Helen were quite creative and imaginative as parents, I'm afraid these qualities hadn't done the firm of Parsley & Parsley much good. In the early days of the firm they had been very successful, and everybody liked the weird and unusual buildings they designed, but their fortunes had, like Ken and Lily Sprout's, declined over the years. At the moment they only had one client, a proposed new factory in the Snudsley area, but one client really wasn't enough to keep them in the black.

Still they couldn't shut off their brains, and just like Ken Sprout, Clive was always thinking of new ideas that would make their fortunes. Sometimes he thought he might try to design some handy little gadget that no one had ever thought of before, but he usually got so carried away with all the fiddly bits and bobs of his new ideas that he completely lost track of the the thing's usefulness.

For example: once, when he was younger, he was in New York on a business trip, and he was in a great rush to pack, and forgot to bring almost everything. Well, he was due for a meeting, and he had to call up the number for *Time-of-Day* to find out if he would be late or not. Of course he forgot to do it and he ended up being late for the meeting. So now, years later, when he had little else to do, he decided to improve the lives of everyone who was forced to rely on calling *Time-of-Day* and began to design a small device that would free humanity from its tyranny.

"You see," he explained to Rennie one evening, "it's a mechanical device, terribly small, which you program with these little buttons here."

It was a little box-like thing, with tiny buttons, about two inches across, and made of some sort of dark and shiny metal.

"Mmm, hmm," said Rennie.

"Say you have an important business meeting at 2:04 p.m. You merely program the 'Time-Phone Device' at the beginning of the day," continued Clive excitedly, "and you input each moment when it will be crucial for you to know the time — in this case you decide that it will take ten minutes to get to the meeting, so you program it for 1:54 p.m. The 'TPD' emits, at each pre-programmed moment, a loud peep, reminding you to call the *Time-of-Day* and get the proper time. Clever, eh?"

Rennie looked at her father's beaming face for a moment.

"Dad, two things," she said. "First, nobody calls *Time-of-Day* anymore. I think they discontinued that service pretty much everywhere, a long time ago."

Clive's face fell slowly, and he looked at her for a moment with glazed eyes.

"And what's the other thing?"

"Well, wouldn't I just wear a watch?" asked Rennie.

Clive looked sadly down at the limp little device in his hand.

"Ah," he said at last. "Ah yes. You might have a point there."

Needless to say, with ideas like the "Time-Phone-Device", the money wasn't exactly rolling in at the Parsley house, and for some time Clive and Helen had been tossing around the idea of renting out some of their large office space to another architectural firm, just to have a bit of extra income to tide things over.

Now, you might be wondering how girls with such different lives and backgrounds and personalities could get along at all, let alone become best friends. Well, Rennie and Velly didn't have much in common, but they *did* share some very important traits — they were almost always bored, they loved a good joke, and they were convinced that they were much cleverer than everybody else.

Of course, they met at school, and this is how.

It so happened that for a time Velly had to go to the Biology Lab every afternoon with a dish of food for Mr. Sticky, the enormous porcupine that was kept there in a cage. Mr. Sticky was once a baby porcupine that the Biology lab had raised as an experiment, but now that he was full grown he had become a sort of mascot for the Science Department. He needed feeding every day, and there was always a student or two who was willing to give him his dinner after school, though Velly had been the only volunteer for a while.

One day she entered the Lab and was surprised to find another girl already there, calmly feeding Mr. Sticky with bits of leftover fish sticks.

"Ah," said the strange girl, looking up at Velly, "the

regular food, lovely. I'm not sure he cares for fish sticks, and I don't blame him."

"Who are you?" said Velly.

"Renate Parsley," said the girl, "but everyone calls me Rennie. You're Velly Sprout, I think?"

"How do you know that?"

Rennie pointed to a piece of paper pinned up over Mr. Sticky's cage.

MR. STICKY
FEEDING SCHEDULE

MON............ Velly Sprout
TUES............ Velly Sprout
WED......... Velly Sprout
THUR......... Velly Sprout
FRI............ Velly Sprout

Velly knelt down beside Rennie and placed the dish of grapes and walnuts in Mr. Sticky's cage, much to the approval of Mr. Sticky. The two girls watched him hungrily gobble for a while, when Velly said —

"Why are you in here?"

"Oh," said Rennie, "I was at a meeting of the Chess Club down the hall, and I was sitting across from Eve

Climber, that tall girl, looking at the boring little castles and the horses, trying to decide if I should employ a Budapest Gambit or the Würzburger Trap, and then it suddenly came to me — *why am I wasting my life*? So I flipped over the board, wandered down the hall here and saw Mr. Sticky. He doesn't seem boring to me. I don't understand anything about animals, but I like them."

"I've had a lot of experience with them," said Velly. "I always end up taking care of animals, it seems. But I love them, too, I must admit."

"Do you think," said Rennie, "that I could come in the afternoon and help you feed him? You must be tired of doing it on your own, and I don't think I'll ever be allowed to go back to the Chess Club."

"Sure," said Velly, smiling.

And so Rennie came to see Velly and Mr. Sticky every afternoon — it was nice, but Rennie was not the sort of person to stay interested in any single thing for very long. After a few days of porcupine duty the two girls had become terrific friends, but Rennie was showing signs of a growing impatience.

"If only he would do something," she would sigh.

"He eats," said Velly.

"Yes, but I mean apart from that," said Rennie. "He has the eating down, but he seems to have no ambitions in other directions."

Velly knelt down by the cage and watched Mr. Sticky in silence.

"We should broaden his horizons," said Rennie in a determined voice. "Do something different with him. Take him for an outing or something."

"We could take him to the beauty parlor," said Velly with a laugh.

"We could dye his prickles," laughed Rennie. "Bright pink!"

They both laughed for a minute, but Velly pointed out that hair dye might hurt him, or even poison him.

"What if," said Rennie, "what if we put something in his cage? Something peculiar? And nobody would know where it came from, and everyone would get very excited, and then we could stand back and have a good laugh."

"Like what sort of something?"

"I don't know. A shoe. A doll, maybe. Or a toy train."

"No," said Velly smiling, "I know. An egg."

"An egg?"

"Listen," said Velly excitedly, "I have a neighbor who has some ducks, and my mom gets fresh eggs from him all the time for the muffins. I could get one that is about to hatch, and we could put it in his cage."

You could tell by the gleam in her eye that Rennie liked the idea, but she was also a little worried.

"But wouldn't he just eat the egg, or the duckling?" she asked. "I hate to think of the little duck, if it hatches, getting chewed up by a porcupine."

"Oh he wouldn't," said Velly. "Mr. Sticky only eats fruits and nuts really. And besides, we would be here every day. We could keep an eye on him."

"Would the cage be warm enough to hatch the egg?"

"They keep it quite warm in here for Mr. Sticky," said Velly, "even at night. And we could tuck the egg in his bedding, over to the side. He probably won't even know it's there. He doesn't move around much."

Rennie considered for a moment, and then looked with a new respect at her friend.

"Love it!" she said.

And so, two days later a perfect, round, white egg was found in Mr. Sticky's cage, much to the amusement of the other children and much to the puzzlement of Mrs. Foam, the Biology teacher. And two days after that, when the egg hatched, and when from it emerged a fuzzy little duckling, there was pandemonium in the classroom.

It seemed to everyone that somehow Mr. Sticky had actually given birth to a duckling; a perfectly healthy duckling. It was completely incredible, the biggest thing to hit the Snudsley School in ages. The little duck was immediately removed from the cage, though Velly had been right — judging from the way he continued to sleep and eat, the entire incident seemed to have no effect whatever on Mr. Sticky himself.

Some students started a petition, asking that Mr. Sticky should henceforth be known as Ms Sticky, since only ladies could lay eggs; but it was pointed out by some other kids that since Mr./Ms/Mrs. Sticky had laid a duck egg, that proved that he/she was actually a duck, and therefore should be called something like Mrs. Beaky or Ms Feathers.

A qualified Biology teacher like Mrs. Foam knew perfectly well that Mr. Sticky had *not* laid an egg, but she didn't actually know what had happened, and she didn't know how to deal with the little duckling now that it had somehow, mysteriously, arrived.

"Would anyone like to take it home and take care of it?" she asked the class.

All the children *wanted* to take the yellow puffball home with them, but almost every one of them either already had a pet, or had parents who wouldn't like the idea.

"Couldn't we let it go free," asked one boy, "down by the Drip?"

"It hasn't got an actual mother, and it's far too little to be able to take care of itself," said Mrs. Foam. "Isn't anyone interested?"

In the end Velly volunteered, since at the moment she didn't have any pets at home, and she didn't think that Ken and Lily would mind having a duck around the place (since they used to have about forty), so she and Rennie put the duckling in a shoebox and took it home that afternoon.

"What should we call him?" asked Rennie.

"I think he looks like he's called Quacky," said Velly.

"Won't he end up being a lot of trouble?" asked Rennie, lifting the lid of the box and peeking in. There was an affectionate *peep*. "He's cute but what does he eat?"

"I sort of remember that I used to feed the ducks in

our back yard a mush of ground up snails and hard-boiled eggs," said Velly. "On toast."

"You're kidding . . ."

"No, it sounds weird, but it's just what ducks like. In any case, don't worry, I'll take care of him over at my house."

"That's good," said Rennie. "I think he's very interesting but I wouldn't know the first thing about taking care of him."

"Trust me, I know how," said Velly. "and besides, how much trouble can a little duckling be?"

❖ ❖ ❖ ❖ ❖

All in all, the Mr. Sticky-Quacky prank was a very important one for Rennie and Velly. It had gone so well that they quickly realized that, if only they were clever enough to think of things so silly that no one else would ever think that anyone would be silly enough to think of them — if that makes any sense — well, it was perfectly possible to pull any sort of prank and get away with it. And have an enormous amount of enormous fun to boot.

So they decided to start their own club after school, which they hoped would sound so dull that no one would join, and then they could have an excuse to get together to plan further little events like Mr. Sticky and the Egg. Rennie came up with *The Snudsley School Boiled Broccoli Afternoon Club*, while Velly's contribution was *The Snudsley School Society for Lint and Dust Preservation*.

"But those might actually attract people," said Rennie. "You know, weird people . . ."

"Let's look on the internet," said Velly.

After a bit of research they decided that *The Snudsley After School Network Phase Payment Analysis Protocol Club* would be the most boring and unattractive club name on the face of the earth, and they were right. Nobody joined, and they were left on their own, in their own empty classroom, every Thursday afternoon.

And that was how *The Snudsley Suggester* was born. Before too long they hit upon the idea of writing and circulating their own school newspaper, filled with all kinds of made-up stories and ridiculous suggestions to the students. They would write it all week long, and then print it up on Thursday afternoon on the old copy machine that was there in the room. Then they would watch people's reactions from a distance and not have to do anything themselves. It had always worked fantastically well, and they had no intention of stopping.

And while the two girls were busy doing that, Quacky was busy eating and growing, and in a short time the little duckling had grown into a great big fat adult duck. Not only that, but it was quite obvious when Quacky began to lay eggs od her own that *he* was actually a *she* — a lovely lady duck with soft eyes and silvery-white plumage.

"We'll have to find a new name for her," said Velly one day. "It strikes me that 'Quacky' is more of a boy's name."

"How about — 'Mrs. Elizabeth Henderson'?" asked Rennie.

"Why?"

"It's unusual," explained Rennie. "Never before in the history of the world has there been a duck named 'Mrs. Elizabeth Henderson'."

"You've got a point."

Of course, Mrs. Henderson was a very nice duck, and very well behaved, generally, but she had a deep and fevered love for Rennie. Even though Velly took care of her day and night, she adored Rennie. Velly thought that Mrs. Henderson even considered Rennie to be her mother, but it couldn't be proved.

Whenever Mrs. Henderson saw Rennie she went completely mad with joy; flapping and squawking, and hopping up and down, and throwing feathers around —

— and *that's* why, one afternoon, someone called Mrs.
Henderson was able to interrupt Rennie and Velly at the
Sprout's dining table.

Three

"Get this crazy duck away from me!" shouted Rennie, and Velly had to reach across the table and scoop up Mrs. Henderson in her arms. She tossed the duck quickly out the back door, where it fluttered into the yard and began to look for worms.

"Now," said Velly, "back to Larp. The super important third thing was . . ."

"I never thought I would live in a world," muttered Rennie, "where I could say 'Get this crazy duck away from me!' and it would actually mean something."

"Rennie!"

"Yes? What?" said Rennie. "I'm sorry, I got confused. The third thing — yes . . ."

"We ought to go to the supermarket on Main Street,"

explained Velly, "the one next to the statue of Snudsley. We'll check out the peanut butter brands and where they are on the shelf. We have to be able to reach them easily, you know — not too high and not too low."

"And it wouldn't hurt to know the layout of the store really well," agreed Rennie, "so we can get in and get out quickly."

"Right," said Velly. "Let's get moving!"

It wasn't a long walk to their local supermarket, and of course they had both been there a thousand times, but they had never really considered just how many brands of peanut butter there were.

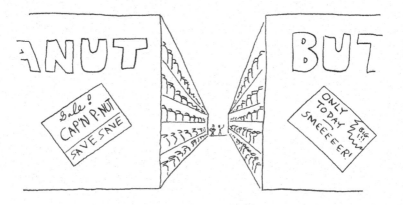

"Amazing," said Rennie, standing in bewilderment before the array of different jars. "Where do we start?"

"Just start at one end, I guess," said Velly.

"Okay," said Rennie, "what about this one? Nut-Tastic?"

"The label is too small," said Velly. "How about Smeeeeeer?"

"The label is good, but the jar has a funny shape," said Rennie. "It might be hard to make the switch. Oh, there's this one — Pea-Licious."

"Or this one — Cap'n P. Nutt?"

"The letters on that one are pretty complicated," said Rennie expertly. "We need something simpler. How about Rich 'N' Gluey?"

"I hate Rich 'N' Gluey," said Velly, "but there's always the smug healthy gourmet brand — Nuts From the Underground. How about that one?"

"That one uses some kind of fancy-schmancy paper for the label," said Rennie after examining it. "I'm not sure we could duplicate it."

"Right," said Velly.

It looked as though the Larp prank might be more complicated than they had thought, and Velly was almost ready to give up, when Rennie lifted a familiar jar off the shelf — a jar which bore the famous orange-and-black label depicting Squee the Squirrel.

"SPREAD-O!" they cried.

"SPREAD-O will be perfect!" said Velly

"I should have thought of that one at the first," said Rennie. "Mom and dad are designing the new SPREAD-O factory out in Snudsley West."

"Really? The new SPREAD-O factory? I've been reading about it in *The Snudslian*. It's a huge project, worth something like a jillion billion dollars for the town."

"I wish it would make mom and dad a jillion billion dollars," said Rennie. "I overheard the two of them talking last night — if no new commissions come up after the factory is complete, we may have to move out."

"Really?"

"Either that," said Rennie, "or rent out the back part of the house as office space."

"My mom and dad's muffin business is sinking too," said Velly. "Mom told me we might have to sell our house as well and move someplace cheaper."

"Move out of your lovely funny house? What would happen to all the things on the walls?"

"I — I don't know," said Velly softly, "I honestly never thought about it before . . ."

"Well, if you had to move, where would you live?"

"I don't know that either," said Velly. "It won't be as nice, wherever it might be, that's for sure. It might not even be in Snudsley."

"Oh well, cheer up, Vel," said Rennie, trying to smile. "It's when things are at their darkest and most hopeless that pointless and stupid pranks come to the rescue. Focus on *Operation Larp* and you'll lose the blues."

"I guess so . . ."

"So anyway, my point was, that my parents have lots of official SPREAD-O folders and corporate brochures lying around the house just now."

"Good," said Velly, feeling a bit more cheerful. Rennie was right — working on *Operation Larp* didn't actually solve any problems but it made her feel better.

"That kind of thing might come in handy when we

need to match some of the artwork and letters on the new label."

"Let's buy a jar," said Rennie, "and get started!"

So they bought a jar of SPREAD-O, and brought it back to Velly's house. Just as they were walking up they saw the front door fly open, and a small group of people began to stream out, with Ken smiling and shaking each of them by the hand.

"Then I can count on you all?" asked Ken.

"Ban the butter!" said one fellow. "I'm in!"

"Squash the squirrel!" said another.

Ken grinned and waved, and then went back into the house. The people all walked away down the sidewalk, chattering amongst themselves.

"Who was that?" asked Rennie.

"Goodness knows," said Velly. "I don't ask anymore."

Once inside the house, they went over to the office corner, which was next to the kitchen zone, and Velly switched on the computer. Rennie decided to remove the label from the jar of SPREAD-O using steam from the teakettle, which was really quite a task what with Mrs. Henderson about. As soon as the duck saw Rennie she hopped up on the counter next to her, and was trying to peck at both the kettle and the arm of Rennie's sweater.

"Quack," said Mrs. Henderson.

"Honestly what is *wrong* with this duck?" said Rennie, trying to brush Mrs. Henderson away as if she were an enormous gnat. "I don't understand what she wants. What what what do you *want*?"

"Quack quack," answered Mrs. Henderson.

"It's nothing to do with me," sniffed Velly, tapping away at the computer. "She thinks that you are her mom, that's all."

"Quack."

"But what am I supposed to do about it?"

"Maybe she wants to learn how to lay an egg," sug-

gested Velly. "You have to teach her how."

"I have to do *WHAT*?" began Rennie, but at that moment they heard a knock at the front door, and Ken went to answer it.

"Hi Mr. Sprout," they heard a small voice say. "Can me and Rumba and Soapy come and see Rennie and um Velly and Mrs. Henderson?"

"Cripes, it's Abigail!" gasped Rennie.

Velly made wild arm and face movements to her father, trying to indicate that Abigail was the last person in the world they wanted to see, but then she heard Ken say —

"Why of course, Abigail, come right in. They're all in the kitchen area."

"Hurry," said Velly, gathering up everything off the table. "Toss all of this junk into your backpack!"

Rennie took the peanut butter jars and the labels and stuffed them all in, along with the brochures, just as Abigail reached the table.

"Hi Velly. Hi Rennie. Can I play with Mrs. Henderson?"

Abigail was quite attached to Mrs. Henderson, though her idea of "playing" was usually nothing more than thrusting Soapy and Rumba into Mrs. Henderson's face and squeaking. Sometimes Mrs. Henderson would tolerate this, and sometimes not. Today, she didn't.

"Quack quack QUACK QUACK QUACK!" screamed the duck, and she fluttered and flapped her wings, and hid behind Rennie for protection.

"Velly," said Abigail, "how come Mrs. Henderson likes Rennie better than you? Is it true Rennie is Mrs. Henderson's mom? What are you doing there?"

"I don't know," said Velly, "not really, and it's none of your business."

"Here, Abigail," said Rennie as she pulled the honking mass of feathers from behind her back, "you take her outside to play, okay?"

"Okay," agreed Abigail — hanging around with Mrs. Henderson was the only thing she enjoyed more than hanging around with Rennie and Velly. The little girl and the duck waddled out into the back yard where Ken was busy in the garden shed.

"Why *does* she like you more than me, actually?" asked Velly after she had gone. "I feed her and take care of her and clean up after her, after all."

"Beats me. I don't encourage her" said Rennie. "It's no secret that I can't understand the animal one little bit. My idea of 'what-to-do-with-a-duck' is limited to roasting tins and chestnut stuffing. I don't want to be the bird's mother."

Velvet was silent for a moment.

"You probably will have to teach her to lay an egg, though, one of these days," she said.

The teakettle began to whistle, and so Rennie pulled the jar of SPREAD-O out of the backpack and Velly returned to the keyboard of her computer. Steaming off the label was the work of a minute, and after she was done, she brought it over to Velly. The two girls scanned the label and began to work at altering it in the computer screen.

"The letters have to look *exactly* the same," said Rennie. "The SPREAD-O letters are really distinctive."

"Right," agreed Velly. "Luckily, both 'peanut butter' and 'Larp' have letters in common — the *A*, the *R*, and the *P*. I can take those from the label we have and just rearrange them. We just need to come up with an *L*."

She clicked a few keys and the new label began to take shape on the computer display; it looked exactly like the

SPREAD-O peanut butter label except it said "arp" where it used to say "peanut butter". But Velly flipped through some of the company's brochures that Rennie had brought, and soon found an *L* from the word *LUSCIOUS* that seemed to fit. She scanned it, tapped a few more keys, and there it was — a very official-looking label for SPREAD-O brand Larp.

"Take a look at that," said Velly proudly.

"Perfect," said Rennie smiling. "How many labels shall we begin with?"

"Oh, no more than twenty or so," said Velly, "until we see how quickly and easily we can change them."

"Roger."

Later that evening, after Abigail had gone home, the two girls sat at Velly's dining table, feeding Mrs. Henderson with little bits of the boiled-egg-snail mixture. Velly had remembered right, that was indeed Mrs. Henderson's favorite food. While they fed her under the table, they worked out when they should actually start changing labels.

"Obviously," said Rennie, "we ought to start fairly soon, and on a weekend day. This project will take some time, and we can't afford to miss any school. We don't want to get into more trouble before we even get started."

"Exactly," said Velly, "and I think we should get going early in the morning, before the store gets too crowded."

"That's a good point," said Rennie. "Basically we have

to get in and paste twenty labels on twenty jars of peanut butter — that should take less than three minutes. But we have to do it without looking conspicuous. Now, I've been thinking about this, and in my opinion we ought to be disguised."

"Disguised? How? You mean like clowns or princesses or something?"

"Of course not, Velvet," said Rennie patiently, "I said we ought *not* to look conspicuous. If you're disguised as a clown or a princess you can't do *anything* without looking conspicuous — you can't even buy a box of Kleenex without looking conspicuous."

Just then Ken burst in through the back door, looking very excited and holding a small mixing bowl in front of him. Velly hastily placed a large envelope over the sheet of Larp stickers they had just printed.

"Ladies," he said dramatically, "I want you two to be the first to try — *this*." With a flourish he dipped a spoon

into the bowl and held it out to them. There was something in the spoon — something glisteny and orangey-purple and quivery.

"Rennie, will you be the first to try?" he breathed.

"I wouldn't be a bit surprised," sighed Rennie. She closed her eyes and cautiously took the spoon into her mouth.

"Now be honest," said Ken, "be *brutally* honest . . ."

Rennie swallowed, and forced a ghastly smile.

"Oh," she choked, "it's — it's wonderful."

Ken's smile fell and he looked at her with disappointment.

"Please, Renate," he said. "I said be *honest*."

"Oh," said Rennie. "Well in that case, what I meant to say was, 'It's completely horrifying'. What the heck is that stuff anyway?"

"That's better," said Ken, his smile returning. "It's my latest Gourmet Veg-Spread — Rasberry-Asparagus Jam. But not quite a success, I gather?" He didn't seem upset — in fact Ken was quite used to his recipes needing ten, twenty, sometimes even fifty stages of refinement before people could bear to even sit next to them, let alone swallow them.

"Not a success, to say the very least," said Rennie. "I doubt that I will be able to get rid of the taste until late next week."

"Now that's too bad," sighed Ken. "Perhaps a bit less vinegar?"

"A bit less of that," said Rennie, "and perhaps a bit less

everything. Nothing at all of everything, in fact."

"Dad, I have to tell you something," interrupted Velly.

"What?"

"It's a new rule," she continued. "You must never ever let Abigail Braintree into the house, for any reason whatsoever, when Rennie and I are in here."

"Why on earth not?" asked Ken, sucking thoughtfully on his spoon, and considering the flavor of his Rasberry-Asparagus Jam. "She's a cute kid."

"It's because," said Rennie significantly, *"we're doing something."*

Most parents of young girls, hearing one of them utter a sentence like this, would instantly pull out all their hair with worry and suspicion. But Ken's mind was far away in Veg-Spread Land, and all he said, as he rose to go, was —

"Oh, all right. Fine. Well, I'm off to the Spread Shed. Thanks for giving the jam a try, and good luck with the um, with the um, with the thing . . ."

He wandered off into the jumble of objects, and disappeared.

"What did he mean," whispered Rennie after he had gone. "'The um the um thing'? Do you think he knows what we're up to?"

"Who knows what my father knows? Anyway it was you who said *'we're doing something'*, like the mad scientist in a horror movie," said Velly. "But don't worry, he didn't notice anything. His brain is adrift in an ocean of Veg-Spreads. I wish he would hurry up and invent some sort of condiment that people could eat without getting sick."

"Maybe it's just the first stage in a Grand Process," said Rennie. "Maybe he will keep making these spreads, each one horrider and horrider than the last, until he comes out the other side of the horridosity tunnel and it will be flavorful and yummy."

"He had better," said Velly, "or we will have to move."

"Hmm . . ." Rennie said thoughtfully.

"Well, now, back to Larp" continued Velly. "Now, about our disguises. If not clowns, what do you think we should dress up as?"

"Well, get this — as boys."

"Boys?"

"Think about it," said Rennie excitedly. "We could wear big parkas, baggy pants and sneakers, and baseball caps. We could push our hair up under the caps, and everyone would think we were boys."

"Okay . . ." said Velly.

"Then, after the Larp switcheroo is discovered, if anyone *had* noticed something funny going on in the peanut butter aisle, they would put the blame on two boys. And two boys no one would recognize because no one had ever seen — them — be — fore —"

There was a long silence. Rennie had suddenly stopped

talking, and seemed to be staring at a pair of antique auto horns, a snood, and a watercolor picture of *The Spirit of St. Louis* that were hanging on the wall.

"Rennie?"

"That's it," said Rennie at last, very softly.

"That's what," asked Velly suspiciously, "exactly?"

Rennie had a wild, happy look in her eye, and Velly groaned. What next? She thought. She knew what that look usually meant — more mischief and more worry and more fretting and more stomach aches. But she was wrong about Rennie this time.

"Mr. Sprout!" shouted Rennie at last. "Mr. Sprout! Come over here please, because I — HAVE — IT!"

"You have what?" asked Ken, running over.

"Yes, what?" asked Velly suspiciously.

"I have," said Rennie carefully, "the solution to everyone's problem. And the solution is this —

"You Sprouts need to move to a cheaper place," she explained, "and we Parsleys need to rent out some of our house to make ends meet. So why don't you all move in with us? You can stay in town, rent your house instead of sell-

ing it, and my parents can rent their extra space to people they know instead of strangers. They make money, and you save money. And after everyone is back on their feet again, perhaps we can all get our houses back and go back to the way things are now. It's a perfect plan; balanced, economical, well-considered, touched with may I say genius, and I really can't imagine why you would say no."

"Quack," agreed Mrs. Henderson from under the table.

And in fact, no one did say "no". In fact everyone was quite impressed that Rennie had come up with such a clever and helpful idea.

The Parsleys agreed that it would be the best thing for everyone if Ken and Lily and Velly moved into the extra office space in the back of Drip Meadows, and the Sprouts agreed to rent out their own house to some nice people from Des Plaines, Illinois who promised that they would take good care of the place and wouldn't change a thing. They spent the next week packing, and the last thing Velly took with her was a large, old-fashioned wicker hatbox from the wall above the oven — because since it was roomy and had a sturdy wooden handle, she thought it would make the perfect duck-carrier for Mrs. Henderson. She put the duck into it, and she found she was right.

So very soon the van from *The Muffin Company* pulled up outside the offices of *Parsley & Parsley*, Drip Meadows, Snudsley, and the Sprouts popped out. Ken and Lily opened the back and started to unload dozens of different-sized crates and boxes onto the sidewalk.

"Let me give you a hand," said Clive, "I can show you where we can store all of this."

"Thanks, Clive," said Ken, "that would be swell. There's a lot!"

There was indeed a lot, a whole lot, and it took the six of them about an hour to empty the van and stack all the boxes in the garage, the living room, and the kitchen.

"Certainly a lot of boxes, Ken," said Helen. "What do you have in here?" She pointed to a neat stack of boxes with the words FORGO SPREAD-O printed on them.

"Some stuff for the protest I'm planning," beamed Ken,

"against the new SPREAD-O factory they're going to build in town. We've got everything!"

"What?" said Clive, and he opened a box and began pulling out sheets of paper.

"Petitions!" he gasped. "Flyers! Brochures! Lapel buttons!"

"All with the same message," explained Ken. "No SPREAD-O in Snudsley. Look, I even have these baseball caps we can give away . . ."

He took two white baseball caps from a box and playfully put one on Clive's head, and another on Helen's. The caps had the name SPREAD-O printed on them with a big red "X" through it.

"You can keep those," said Ken. "Anyway, the whole town's going to pull together and formally protest the building of this new, big, horrid, noisy, smelly factory!"

"Ken," said Clive, "Helen and I are, in fact, the architects of the new SPREAD-O factory."

"And I'm sure it will be a *beautiful* big, horrid, noisy, smelly factory!" exclaimed Ken, snatching back the two baseball caps and stuffing them into the box.

"Sorry, never mind about me, Clive, Helen," he said nervously, "I'll keep these things sealed up, don't worry, you won't ever see them . . ."

All the boxes were swiftly unpacked, and everyone more or less settled in, without too much trouble. Velly's family didn't have very much in common with the Parsleys, but they did share this one thing; the Parsleys didn't like walls and doors either, and had a house full of big open spaces. Ken and Lily and Velly soon felt at home in the large, airy living zone.

"I think Velly should stay in my room," said Rennie in the afternoon, as a sort of announcement, while everyone was running around and putting things away. "She can sleep in my bed, just like she does when she stays overnight."

Ken and Lily looked at one another, and then at Velly,

who was on the floor and putting her own bed together with a screwdriver.

"How would that be, dear?" asked Lily.

"Um — fine, I guess," said Velly.

"Oh good then it's *all settled*," said Rennie in a loud voice, and grabbed Velvet by the arm and began pulling her towards her bedroom. "Come along, Velly, I'll show you where it is," she said.

"But I know where it is . . ." said Velly.

Once inside her room Rennie shut the door carefully behind her.

"You know," said Velly, "I actually have my own bed. It was that large and flattish metal thing out there, the one with the mattress."

"If we stay together in the same room," explained Rennie, "it will be much easier for us to carry out phase one of *Operation Larp*. Or had you forgotten?"

"I hadn't forgotten, exactly," stammered Velly. "I'm just thinking — oh I don't know. Everything is so up in the air right now. No money, our families living together, no *Suggester*. I don't think we should take stupid and irresponsible risks. What if everything goes wrong? I know that part of the plan was to get caught eventually, but . . ."

"It wasn't part of the plan, it was the whole point of the plan," said Rennie. "It was how we decided to get back at the Principal. In any case, taking stupid and irresponsible risks is our trademark. It's just another good reason for you to stay in my room. That way I can make sure you take as many stupid and irresponsible risks as I do."

"But Rennie —"

"And it will be much simpler with you staying here in my house, because now that Abigail doesn't live down the street, we don't have to worry as much about her butting in anymore."

"You're right," said Velly thoughtfully, "there's no real problem anymore with Abigail . . ."

Just then a strange, almost silent whispering — no, a sort of brushing or quiet tapping — came from outside the bedroom window. Since they had just been talking of Abigail, the same thought ran through both of their minds.

"No, it couldn't be," said Rennie as she opened the window. "Could it?"

Suddenly the room was filled with a chaotic flurry of wings and webbed feet and clacking beak.

It wasn't Abigail.

"QUAACK!" screamed Mrs. Henderson, overcome with joy at having found her mother once again. She pounced on Rennie with the fury of a lonely duck returning home after an epic journey.

"Good grief!" cried Rennie, flailing her arms. "Get this absurd bird off me!"

Velly couldn't help bursting into laughter. It had been

a melancholy day, and she knew she would miss her own house, but she thought that maybe — just maybe — it wouldn't be so bad living at DRIP MEADOWS after all.

❖   ❖   ❖   ❖   ❖

Now, say you happened to find yourself in Snudsley on a bright and cheerful Sunday morning, and say you happened to be walking down Main Street at precisely ten minutes to nine. Then you might have seen, as you passed the big bronze statue of General Cuthbert Snudsley, two boys in parkas, sneakers and baseball caps immediately beneath it, whispering together in excited voices.

"Labels ready?" said Rennie.

"Ready," said Velly, clutching the folder tightly to her.

"You understand what to do?" asked Rennie for the hundredth time. "You get a jar from the shelf and hand it to me. I stick on the label and hand the jar back to you, at which point you —"

"Put it back on the shelf, yes I know," said Velly. "But Rennie, I'm — I'm — I'm . . ."

"You're what?"

"I'm still not sure I can go through with it," said Velly nervously.

"Oh no," said Rennie, rolling her eyes, "here we go again, right on schedule."

"Maybe you should do it on your own," suggested Velly brightly. "After all, one boy is bound to attract less attention that two boys."

"Forget it," said Rennie, turning Velly around and pushing her towards the doors of the supermarket across the street. "You're not going to chicken out now. Besides I need you to manage the labels while I stick them on the jars. Since I don't have four arms, you're absolutely vital to the procedure. So stop whimpering and let's just go."

And they went.

The moment they entered the store through the front

door they saw a man in a necktie (he must have been the store manager) arranging some plastic boxes of clothes pins into a pyramid by the front door.

"Mornin' boys!" he said.

"Morning!" responded the girls, in the best deep voices they could manage.

They hurried on straight ahead. On their right were the bread and cheese counters, and on their left the aisles fanned out one after the other like office blocks.

"On to the peanut butter section," said Rennie,

"Down the next aisle," whispered Velly.

They turned the corner hurriedly — and then stopped in horror.

"Oh no. It can't be . . ."

But it was. They had spotted a little girl and her mother, looking at the jams and marmalades, directly between them and the shelves of peanut butter.

"It's Abigail and her mom!"

"What'll we do now?"

"Quit, I think," said Velly, cheerfully turning on her heels and making for the exit. "Quit quit quit. Forget the whole thing."

"Not on your life," whispered Rennie fiercely. "She won't recognize us — we're disguised as boys, remember?"

Rennie dragged Velly by the hood to where Abigail, Soapy and Rumba were discussing the merits of strawberry jam over apricot.

"Shame about the team," said Velly huskily.

"Yeah, yeah," said Rennie, "still got a chance though."

"Grrzs!! Strawberry is better!! Bgbyhghb — don't like ape-cot!!" said Abigail, which the two girls took to mean that she indeed did not recognize them, and together they breathed a sigh of relief.

And now they were there, directly in front of the peanut butter section. Velly looked carefully around her — no one was there except for Abigail and her mom, and they had already chosen their jam and were pushing their cart away into the next aisle.

"Brilliant disguises," she said. "Abigail didn't bat an eye."

"Perfect," said Rennie, "let's get to work."

They turned back to the shelves, but —

"Wait," gasped Velly. "It's gone!"

"What's gone?"

"SPREAD-O!" said Velly.

It was true. All the other familiar brands were in their places, and there was a little card on the edge of the shelf which read *SPREAD-O $2.25*, but not one jar of the stuff was to be seen.

"Drat," said Rennie, "I hadn't thought of that."

"It's sold out," said a small voice behind them.

They turned around and saw no one — until they looked down. Abigail, Soapy and Rumba were back, and looking up at them.

"It's all gone but I like peanut butter," she continued as they stared down at her. "I like all kinds. Smeeeeeer, and Pea-Licious, and Rich 'N' Gluey, and that other one what's

it called. Rumba doesn't like Smeeeeeer, but I like Smeeeeeer. I made Soapy eat Rich 'N' Gluey, didn't I Soapy? He got sick and threw up." And she woggled Soapy and made loud throwing-up sounds.

"Um, yeah," mumbled Rennie and Velly.

"But SPREAD-O is best. We just got the last jar of it. It goes with strawberry. I like SPREAD-O. But Soapy doesn't like SPREAD-O. Do you like SPREAD-O?"

Rennie and Velly had no idea what to say, so they tried again with —

"Um. Yeah."

"Me too," said Abigail. "I like SPREAD-O. We just got the last jar so bye!" And with that, she left the girls and ran back after her mom, disappearing around the corner of the aisle.

"Well, that's was just about *too scary*," said Rennie, her voice shaking. "Maybe you were right after all. She'll never leave us alone. Even if she doesn't know who we are she won't leave us alone. We'll have to try again some other time."

"Not so fast," said Velly, perking up her ears. "Hear that?"

It was the sound of wheels. Little metallic squeaky wheels.

"What is it?" asked Rennie, but Velly didn't have to answer, because at that moment they saw a stock boy came around the corner pushing an enormous metal cart full of SPREAD-O peanut butter jars.

"Oops," they both said under their breath. Of course what they *thought* was "hooray", but they had to say "oops", because if the stock boy was going to restock the SPREAD-O shelf, it would mean that they would have to get out of there very quickly and the come back when he was through and no one else was around. As the morning hours grew later and later, the supermarket would get more and more crowded — they didn't have too much time to waste.

Without a second thought they pulled their caps down, squeezed past the stock boy and his cart, and dashed around the corner of the aisle into the salty snacks section.

"That was close," said Velly. "What do you think, should we hang around or try another day?"

"We're so perfectly prepared," said Rennie, "I'd hate to give up just yet. Let's spend some time wandering around the store and then try once more in a little while. If that doesn't work, I am willing to postpone the first raid to another day."

Velly didn't agree or disagree. In fact she couldn't say anything, because at that moment she saw something that she was perfectly certain she would never have to see as long as she lived on the planet Earth.

It was the sight of a gigantic bag of potato chips walking towards her, holding a platter of smaller yet similar bags of the same chips.

"Hi," said the bag as soon as it was close enough. "I'm

Carl, the giant Crumbly Chips bag. Care to sample some complimentary Crumbly Chips?"

"Yeah, great, free potato chips," said Rennie, grabbing two bags off the platter. "Thanks, Carl."

"You're welcome. Enjoy your Crumbly Chips."

Velly saw that there was a slit in the bag costume so that the person inside could see out, and two large eyes glanced at them both before the bag turned itself awkwardly around and shambled down the aisle towards an old lady with a shopping cart.

"I didn't know you liked Crumbly Chips," whispered Velly.

"I don't," sniffed Rennie, "they're disgusting. But we're not supposed to draw attention to ourselves, remember?"

"Did you see his eyes?" said Velly. "They looked so somber."

"You'd have somber eyes too, if the high point of your whole career was being a huge sack of Crumbly Chips," said Rennie. "Now come on."

They turned back down the aisle and began to head towards the peanut butter section. But the manager was standing at the far end of the aisle and Rennie and Velly thought that he was starting to look at them sort of suspiciously. So they stopped next to the old lady with the shopping cart, who was looking at different cans of canned meat. In order to look more like they were actually shopping, Velly held up a can of deviled ham and pretended to examine the list of ingredients.

"Oh it's perfectly fine," said the old lady.

"What?" said Rennie, not looking at her but at the manager at the end of the aisle.

"That deviled ham that is engrossing your pal, young man," said the old lady. "You see, I know all about deviled ham. My grandfather invented deviled ham. And he inserted it full of wholesomeness, too."

"Uh huh," said Rennie. The manager had moved on and she saw their chance to move on one aisle, so she put Velly's deviled ham back on the shelf and pushed her along down the aisle.

"He never made any money from it, though," shouted the old lady after them, "because Kaiser Wilhelm stole the recipe from him!"

"Crazy as a brick," muttered Rennie as she turned the corner. "How are we supposed to be inconspicuous if things like that keep happening?"

"Maybe we should have been clowns after all," said Velly.

They could see now, from the end of the aisle, that the stock boy had gone, Abigail and her mother had gone, and there were about forty fresh jars of SPREAD-O sitting expectantly on the shelves.

"Now's our chance," whispered Velly.

"Let's get going," said Rennie, but before they took two steps they heard a strange muffled sound behind them.

"Snurf. Oink. Smoky bacon?"

Slowly they turned around to see a large pig in a chef's hat, holding a silver platter, on which were set several little plastic trays with bits of fried bacon in them.

"Good morning, *gentlemen*," said a barely audible voice from somewhere in the vicinity of the pig's mouth. "May I tempt you with some smoky bacon from Oink Acres Farms, thrice voted the finest pig farm in the eastern states by Pig Weekly Magazine?"

"No," stammered Velly, "um — no thanks, man."

"Yeah," added Rennie. "We're like, um, vegetarians."

"Ah," said the pig, "the V-word. Well, we see a lot of that these days — it can't be helped, I suppose. Anyway, thank you for your time, *gentlemen*." And with a slight bow and flourish he disappeared around the corner.

"What did he mean by that?" squeaked Velly. "'*Gentlemen*'. I didn't like how he said it, not one bit! We're sunk now. Do you think he saw through our disguises? Do you?"

"Get a hold of yourself!" said Rennie, shaking Velly by the shoulders. "It's only a pig. Even if he saw that we were girls, who's going to listen to a pig?"

"You're right, you're right . . ."

"Anyway, there's the peanut butter section, and no one else is around."

After all the trouble it had taken them to get there, the actual changing of the labels was simple and quick. Velly handled the labels like she was born to it, and as for Rennie — well, if there ever had been an Olympic event for Peanut-Butter-Label-Sticking-On, she would have won the gold medal. In less than one minute they had pasted on all twenty of their homemade labels. There were some unchanged jars left over, but they pushed those into the back.

"Good," said Rennie. "Let's go!"

"At last," sighed Velly.

As they strode confidently back up the aisle and around the corner, they could see the manager watching them with gradually increasing suspicion. They knew that they had better get out of there fairly quickly, but they didn't want to make a run for it, because that would draw even *more* attention to themselves. No, what they wanted was to slip out, quickly and quietly, without any more mishaps.

And maybe they would have, if it hadn't been for Kevin.

"Hi! I'm a sad acorn, and my name is Kevin. Care for a sample of Sun-Squirt Orange Juice?"

I don't expect you to believe it — in fact even Rennie and Velly couldn't actually *believe* it — but there he was nonetheless. A very large papier-mâché acorn with big teary cartoon eyes standing in the juice aisle, blocking their escape, and holding a tray covered with little cups of orange juice.

"It's really good," he said.

Rennie looked behind her — the manager was looking at them carefully, pointing, and giving instructions to a couple of stock boys, who were also looking at them. Time was running out.

"Why are you an acorn?" she blurted out.

"What?"

"Yes, why *are* you an acorn?" asked Velly, as the two girls forced their way slowly around him. The exit to the street was just a few feet away, and now they had moved to a position where Kevin was between themselves and the manager.

"It doesn't make any sense," said Rennie, as they started to move quickly towards the door.

"I mean" added Velly, "if you sell orange juice you should be an orange, shouldn't you?"

"I know, I know!" yelled Kevin after them. "I said I was a *sad* acorn!"

Unfortunately the supermarket had been designed so that there was no way out except by standing in the lines at the cash registers, so the girls had to squeeze past a line of shoppers before they could leave, and the line they picked happened to contain the old lady, who had piled a great many cans of deviled ham onto the conveyor belt.

"Yes, and the Kaiser made all the money," she was telling the lady behind her. "How do you think he could afford to make all those Zeppelins?"

But at last they made it to the front door. The manager and the two stock boys looked on helplessly as Rennie and Velly shot out the door, into the street, and disappeared into the wide world — a world that now contained *Larp*.

Four

After that, things went a bit more smoothly. Rennie and Velly got better and quicker and smarter — they never again had problems with supermarket managers, or strange old ladies, or talking pigs, and they carefully avoided big bags of potato chips. In fact they soon stopped disguising themselves as boys, since Abigail didn't follow them around anymore, and they knew that they could get into any supermarket and out again in just a few minutes, leaving nothing behind them but a trail of the mysterious Larp. No one ever paid any attention to what they were doing.

Soon they had done all the supermarkets in the Snudsley area, as well as the supermarkets in the neighboring villages of Caketown, Bluffing, and Bolt. One Saturday morning they even replaced the labels on one hundred jars of

SPREAD-O in a big giant hypermarket outside Dollydale. But Rennie and Velly realized, one Tuesday afternoon — about three weeks after they had started *Operation Larp* — that after all that time the original jars they had altered in those first markets had probably all been sold, and they would have to consider how to get back into these same stores and start the whole process over again.

It seemed best to go back at different times of day; for example, if they did the label-switch in the morning at Supermarket X the first time, they would go back at five in the afternoon the second time, just before closing the third time, and so on.

"That means that different employees will be in the store each time we go in, because of the change in shifts, and they won't remember us" explained Velly.

And Velly must have known what she was talking about, because they never had any difficulties, and they never got caught. She stopped being nervous, and Rennie started to think that Operation Larp was turning out to be a lot of fun — too much fun to let themselves get caught, as was their original plan.

But in the meantime, conversations like this one began to take place at more and more breakfast tables in the general area.

DAUGHTER: (noisily) I don't want a peanut butter sandwich, mommy, I want a Larp sandwich!

FATHER: (from behind newspaper) What is she saying? What what what?

MOTHER: She keeps saying "Larp" instead of "peanut butter". It's driving me out of my tree.

DAUGHTER: But it is called "Larp", mommy, and I don't want any horrible old peanut butter!

MOTHER: I bought you a jar of Smeeeeeer just like I always do.

DAUGHTER: No last week you bought SPREAD-O and it was "Larp" and not "peanut butter" and now I have to eat Smeeeeeer peanut butter and I don't want any Smeeeeeer peanut butter I want Larp! SPREAD-O Larp! (begins to whine and wail) Laaaaaaaaaaaarp!

FATHER: (throws paper aside) Great Scott I'm going out!

MOTHER: I'm coming with you!

DAUGHTER: Laaaaaaaaaaarp!

This began to happen with an alarming frequency. Children began to accept Larp into their hearts, even as their parents had no idea at all what was going on. You must understand that the grown-ups didn't notice the change to the label — because it was still orange, still had a picture of Squee the Squirrel on it, and was still in the same place on the supermarket shelf. They just grabbed the jar. They never looked. Velly and Rennie might have named it "SPREAD-O Horse Manure" and I doubt that any adult would have noticed.

However, what parents *do* in fact notice is when their children begin screaming and crying and demanding something nobody has never heard of, and they won't shut up no matter what you say to them. Soon the grown-ups started to notice Larp, too, and started to wonder what was going on. And Rennie and Velly learned rather suddenly that their little prank was getting results — big results.

One afternoon, after a secret label-printing session, Velly was sitting on the bed when she opened the newspaper.

She gasped.

In one split second she felt her heart leap in her chest, up her throat, and out into the back yard.

"R — R — Rennie?" she managed to stammer at last.

"Good heavens, what's wrong?" said Rennie. "You're as white as a ghost, and you're trembling as if you've just seen a ghost, and that's too many ghosts. What's the matter?"

"No ghosts," whispered Velly. "Worse! Page eleven!"

Rennie took the paper, opened it to page eleven, and she too let out a little gasp as she read —

BAFFLING BUTTER BLITZ

SNUDSLEY — Imagine you are fond of a certain strange, pasty substance, made from peanuts, which you might be partial to spreading on a piece of bread for your lunch. You'd be tempted to call it "peanut butter" wouldn't you? After all, millions do — including the people who make the stuff. But you'd be wrong; at least that's according to Leonard Cling, manager of the local supermarket in the small village of Snudsley.

"We noticed it a few weeks ago," the mystified manager explained. "All the jars of SPREAD-O peanut butter suddenly became jars of SPREAD-O Larp. We contacted the SPREAD-O firm, but we never got past the reception lady — she said we were kooks!"

So did the police, whom Cling phoned as soon as he was done opening some cartons of puppy food. But his store was not alone — other supermarkets as far away as Dollydale and Toff reported the same mysterious metamorphosis. The police have no leads but frankly don't seem to care.

"I mean, peanut butter labels?" said a police spokes-

woman. "*We have parking tickets to worry about!*"

Nonetheless they promised to look further into the matter as long as nothing else is going on.

"I think the word 'whoops' might be appropriate at this point," said Rennie calmly, laying the paper down.

"What are we going to do?" asked Velly in a panic. "I mean, now the police are involved."

"Well, we knew that we would get caught eventually," said Rennie, "it was all part of the plan."

"Yes, *caught*", said Velly, starting to froth into a perfect panic, "but not arrested by the CIA! We're in trouble — big deep fat enormous trouble!"

"Get a hold of yourself," said Rennie sternly. "It's not the CIA, it's the local police force of Snudsley. That's three people, tops. And the paper says very clearly that they don't have any leads, and further, that they don't care a button about it."

"Well, yes," agreed Velly, looking at the story again, "I guess that's true."

"I think we are," said Rennie, "in the clear, as they say."

The two girls were then silent, and thoughtful — they might be in the clear, but it was a bit of a shock to discover that their little project had drawn the attention of both the police and the newspapers. They looked at the pile of labels in the middle of the bed.

"What shall we do now?" asked Velly quietly after a time. "Shall we stop for a bit?"

"Stop?" grinned Rennie. "Not *quite* yet. If we stop now everyone will know it was some kind of stupid prank. If we go on, we will really start people wondering. And I must say that this is fun — I'm sort of hoping now that we never get caught. We can think of some other way to get back at that rotten old Box."

"From prison?" said Velly. "That will be a good trick. Don't forget, they will be looking out for us now. If we don't stop, how on earth can we possibly keep from getting caught?"

Rennie leaned forward over the table, and smiled knowingly.

"By *not* stopping," she said, "and by taking even *bigger* and *stupider* risks."

❖　❖　❖　❖　❖

At the very moment that Rennie leaned over the table and said to Velly —

"By taking even *bigger* and *stupider* risks."

— at exactly that precise moment, in a certain very large and high-up-in-the-sky sort of office, in an enormous glass building in an enormous city, far from Snudsley and our two heroines, a certain desk buzzer began buzzing on a certain desk.

"Yes?"

"Pardon me, Mr. Whacker," said a female voice. "But

Squee the Squirrel is here. He says it's urgent."

"Llewellyn Trevellyn? Send him in."

The man snatched his one hand away from the desk intercom, folded it in the other, and began to whirl his thumbs jerkily around one another. He seemed a bit nervous and preoccupied, but then he always seemed that way. Being Weed Whacker, the head of an enormous peanut butter company like SPREAD-O, was anything but relaxing. He certainly didn't look like a relaxed sort of person. He was short and rumpley and looked as though he never had time to comb his thin grey hair. And Mr. Whacker didn't know it yet, but he was about to get even more nervous and preoccupied.

A tall, rather elegant gentleman in a tailored suit, light blue fedora hat and pearl-gray gloves swept into the office and collapsed into one of the chairs.

"Well," he breathed. "It's only total chaos, that's all. Total and utter and sheer and complete and unmitigated chaos!"

"What are you gibbering about, Trevellyn?" asked Mr. Whacker curtly.

"I *do* so wish, Mr. Whacker,"

said the gentleman, "that you would instruct your lovely Miss Limb in the foyer to stop announcing me as Squee the Squirrel. 'Tis but a mask, a costume, 'tis an actor's role, in truth."

"It's been your *only* role for thirty years," snapped Mr. Whacker. "Now what do you want? What's all this blithering about chaos and disaster?"

"What?" asked Mr. Trevellyn. "Noble friend, can it possibly be that you don't know, that you are unaware, that you remain uninformed?"

"Of what, you buffoon?"

"Of —this!" exclaimed Mr. Trevellyn, and he flung a newspaper onto Mr. Whacker's desk, opened to page eleven — and we all know what he read there.

"Cream gravy," gasped Mr. Whacker under his breath, turning gradually paler as he read the article. "Is all this true, Llewellyn?"

"It's worse," sighed Mr. Trevellyn sadly. "I've no inkling how it has happened, but the phenomenon is spreading far beyond the Snudsley area. Last weekend, when I was at a supermarket opening outside Walpole, I distinctly heard the children shouting something like 'Down peanut butter! Up Larp!'."

"No," said Mr. Whacker. "You heard it clearly, even through the squirrel head?"

"Yes, Mr. Whacker," Mr. Trevellyn nodded, *"even through it."*

While Llewellyn Trevellyn buried his face in his hands, Mr. Whacker got up from his desk. He slowly and silently walked around the office, past the framed awards and certificates on the wall; SPREAD-O voted Best Peanut Butter below the Mason-Dixon Line, SPREAD-O contracts with the Navy and Air Force, letters praising SPREAD-O from noted TV stars. Finally he stopped in front of the huge plate glass window and spoke softly.

"What to do, what to do?" he said. "You work all your life to make a product, create a company and dedicate your life to it, and then suddenly, one fine day, everyone starts calling your product by a completely stupid made-up name. It's not something that they prepare you for in business college."

"Who can understand the workings of fate?" asked Mr. Trevellyn, suddenly lifting his face from his hands and springing dramatically to his feet. "'Our remedies oft in ourselves do lie, which we ascribe' — "

"Oh shut up!" said Mr. Whacker, lunging for his desk buzzer, and pressing the button firmly. "It's *sabotage*, that's what it is — it's some weasel at some other peanut butter company trying to ruin me!"

He pointed a firm finger at Mr. Trevellyn, who was once again pale and trembling in his chair.

"Well, they won't get away with it, squirrel," he smiled horribly. "THEY WON'T GET AWAY WITH IT!"

❖　❖　❖　❖　❖

Through his desk intercom Mr. Whacker gave his secretary, Miss Limb, instructions to find out whatever she could about the "Snudsley Crisis", and to bring him the information first thing in the morning. At home that evening, Miss Limb considered a number of information-gathering techniques — an army of spies, phone tapping, specially-aimed satellite discs — before deciding on the technique of reading through a few copies of *The Snudsley Evening Star* and then going to bed.

Mr. Whacker also went home eventually, paced back and forth in his living room, mumbled the word "Larp" several times through gritted teeth, drummed his fingers on the table, paced a bit more, and then he also went to bed — though he didn't sleep much.

The next morning he buzzed for Miss Limb, who swiftly blew into his office with her pad and several issues of the newspaper.

"All right, Limb," sighed Mr. Whacker, "just how bad is it? What have you found out?"

"Details are sketchy at this point, Mr. Whacker," said Miss Limb crisply, unfolding the first newspaper. "The first jars of so-called 'Larp' were discovered a month ago in a Snudsley supermarket. The next jars began to appear a few days later in several other supermarkets, and then in various supermarkets in neighboring towns. There doesn't seem to be any pattern in the supermarkets involved — in the last month nearly every chain has experienced the Larp effect."

"The Larp *plague*, you mean," said Mr. Whacker glumly. "Any suspects?"

"Not yet, sir," said Miss Limb, "in fact the police weren't even sure foul play was involved until a few days ago. Everyone just assumed we were changing the name of the product."

"And it's just us?" asked Mr. Whacker.

"Just SPREAD-O," said Miss Limb.

Mr. Whacker smoldered a bit.

"That just *proves* that it's one of our competitors, trying to ruin our company!" he suddenly cried, jumping out of his chair. "Otherwise why wouldn't jars of Pea-Licious or Cap'n P. Nutt suddenly start turning into jars of Larp?"

"Yes, sir."

"Come to that," said Mr. Whacker, "why wouldn't cans of lime juice and bags of baby wipes and packages of dis-

posable razors become Larp as well? Hmm? I mean, 'Larp' doesn't mean anything."

"I'm sure I don't know sir. But you might be right. It *could* be another peanut butter company."

Mr. Whacker walked over to the big plate glass window again and looked out of it, which was his favorite thing to do when he wanted to think about the injustices that were constantly being heaped upon his peanut butter presidency. His mind raced as he took in the new information Miss Limb had brought him.

"It's Tode over at Nut-Tastic, I'll bet," he mused. "That Tode is a sleazy customer, and he's always had it in for me. Since the Year Dot he's resented the popularity of SPREAD-O, and its incredible success, and now he thinks he'll get his revenge. Well, over my dead body he will!"

"But sir, why is it only happening in Snudsley?"

"Simple!" yelled Mr. Whacker, although Miss Limb was only a few feet away. "Because we are about to build a new SPREAD-O peanut butter factory in Snudsley. It's been approved! It's all set to go! And so now, suddenly, jars of SPREAD-O start being labeled as something called Larp, right in the neighborhood of our lovely new factory. Coincidence? I think not!"

Miss Limb nodded a lot.

"No, Limb," continued Mr. Whacker, "this smells fishy to me — building begins in just a few weeks, and I'll bet

Tode figures that there's no better way to jinx the whole thing than by pulling a ridiculous stunt like this in the very same town."

"Hmm," said Miss Limb, "I must say that the whole thing *does* smell a bit fishy at that."

"It smells about as fishy as — as —" said Mr. Whacker vaguely. "Limb, what's the fishiest thing you can imagine?"

Miss Limb folded up her little pad, and placed it in her lap, and gazed out of the big plate glass window with a dreamy smile.

"When I was little," she began, "we used to go every summer to visit my grandfather, who lived in the country. He loved going fishing, and used to take me out with him onto the lake, just him and me, in his little boat. How well I remember the lush green hills, and the sun glinting off the rippling water. One beautiful summer morning I can recall particularly well, for it was a very productive one, and we rowed back to shore with seven eels, two pike, four perch, another pike, any number of bass and croppies, and a large collection of smelts. We also had several huge bags of frozen prawns, ten cartons of fish sticks and some cans of sardines that we were supposed to deliver to the orphanage down the road on our way home. Oh, and plus my mother had made us tuna sandwiches for lunch.

"And that, Mr. Whacker," she sighed, "is the fishiest thing I can think of."

Mr. Whacker stood up from his chair slowly.

"Well this smells fishier," he said with feeling, "than *even that*."

"Yes, sir . . ."

"Now get that squirrel in here, and call the FBI! This is war, Miss Limb, and it's time to take action!"

Meanwhile, in a different yet similar office, in a different yet similar tall glass building on the other side of the enormous city, Mr. Tode sat smiling at his own different yet similar secretary, Miss Bundle.

You would tend to think that someone named "Mr. Tode" would look rather short and squat and slimy, but that would be wrong in this case. This particular Mr. Tode, who was the president of the Nut-Tastic Peanut Butter Company, was very long and thin, and much younger than his rival at SPREAD-O. His hair glistened like glass, because he put tons and tons of oily goo in it each morning to make it that way. He wore dark grey and dark blue suits that looked very expensive. He smiled all the time — not

in a friendly way, but in a way that sort of gives you the creeps.

"Larp, eh?" he smiled. "Dazzling. Wonderful. Brilliant. It's almost impossible to believe that Whacker could come up with such a winner. Larp. Pure genius. And how long has this been going on, Bundle?"

Miss Bundle, who had been reading from the same newspapers as had Miss Limb, said —

"About a month, sir."

"About a month. Inspired." Mr. Tode smiled quietly to himself and gazed off into space. "Think of it, Bundle," he continued. "You run one of the biggest peanut butter companies in the country, and just at the moment that you begin building a state-of-the-art factory in the Snudsley area, you decide to secretly change the name of your product in that same area — and everyone loves it. Exceptional."

"Yes," agreed Miss Bundle. "Really terrific sir."

"And the only drawback," smiled Mr. Tode, "the only fly in the soup, the only spanner in the works, the only worriment — IS THAT WE DIDN'T THINK OF IT FIRST!"

Miss Bundle squeaked, and jumped up a little bit in the air, but Mr. Tode paid no attention to her as he walked with long steps around his office, talking and smiling as much to himself, it seemed, as to her.

"All right," he said quickly, "Damage Control. War Plan. Priorities. Priority One — we begin changing our Nut-Tastic peanut butter to Nut-Tastic 'Larp'. Call the label department."

"Right," said Miss Bundle, making a careful note in her little pad.

"Second — new mascot. Call a brainstorming meeting for tomorrow morning."

"Mascot meeting morning," said Miss Bundle, "got it."

"New mascot will go to all the Snudsley supermarkets, as well as to the supermarkets in a one hundred mile area surrounding Snudsley. Free samples, local coverage, advertising push — slogan! This! 'A New Look for New Nut-Tastic Larp'."

"New slogan," murmured Miss Bundle.

"Third priority — we hit every newspaper and magazine in the country with a massive advertising campaign. Call the advert boys and tell them to get going — I want at least *two hundred* completely new campaigns on my desk by tomorrow morning or heads will roll."

"Heads," repeated Miss Bundle, still writing. "What about television, sir? Internet ads?"

"Oh yes," said Mr. Tode with his most chilling smile. "Something to consider. Something to ponder. In the end, however, I suspect that such measures will not be necessary. Whacker didn't do anything except change his labels. I promise you, in three days we will have a cute new mascot, a wonderful new product, and we will have ruined SPREAD-O — for good!"

❖ ❖ ❖ ❖ ❖

There were already seven or eight people seated nervously around a big table the next morning, when Mr. Tode strode purposefully into the meeting room. His hair looked even tighter and shinier than usual.

"Right," he snapped. "A new mascot. Ideas. Boom, let's hear from you first."

Mr. Boom fidgeted and then softly said —

"I was thinking of, perhaps, an owl?"

"Owl? Peanut butter?" said Mr. Tode abruptly. "What do owls have to do with peanut butter?"

"W-well," stammered Mr. Boom, "I *like* owls . . ."

"Okay, owls are out," said Mr. Tode. "Next?"

"Say there, chief," grinned a man called Mr. Overcurdle, "how about a tree? A talking tree?"

"A tree?"

"Well, a tree is a plant, and a peanut is a sort of *vegetable*, so I thought . . ."

"Except that peanuts don't grow on trees," smiled Mr. Tode, "they grow on shrubs. You want our New Nut-Tastic Larp Mascot to be a shrub?"

"Well, obviously a *talking* shrub . . ."

"The stupidest idea in the history of the world," said Mr. Tode. "Basket, what did you come up with?"

"Well," said a young woman with wide eyes, "I was thinking of a mouse."

"A mouse," said Mr. Tode slowly. He rocked back in his chair and smiled up at the ceiling. "Well, mice do eat peanuts, I suppose . . ."

"Sure they do," said Miss Basket, who began to feel encouraged.

"And," said Mr. Tode, sitting

up in his chair again, "they are horrid and vile and filthy and dreadful little pests that everyone hates. Next."

"How about a rabbit?" someone suggested.

"No connection to peanut butter."

"A butterfly? A kangaroo?"

"No connection at all," said Mr. Tode testily.

"A warthog? A shark? A marsh-warbler?"

"Completely ridiculous."

"What about — what about — " began a sweaty-looking man at the far end of the table.

"What about what, Waffle?"

"Well," continued the man, "I suppose a *toad* is out of the question . . ."

"Now listen," barked Mr. Tode, "I pay you people a lot of money to come up with ideas, and all you've given me today is the feeblest collection of zoo animals I've ever heard of, with a talking shrub thrown in. I have half a mind to —"

"How about a shrew?" asked a small voice at Mr. Tode's elbow. It belonged to Melanie Snip, one of the newest executives at Nut-Tastic.

"A shrew?"

"Yes," she said. "Shrews are small, mouse-like, and cute — but they don't break into people's cupboards and eat their granola, so people don't hate them. Easy to make talk, easy to cartoon-ize. It's a natural."

"A shrew — named Shirley," said Mr. Tode dreamily. "Or Sherman . . ."

"Or Shawn," whispered Miss Snip, "or Shelly or Shane or Seamus."

"That's it!" cried Mr. Tode. "Get the advertising department to work on designing the mascot. Shane the Shrew is the new face of Nut-Tastic Larp! Snip, you are the now the new Vice-President in charge of Marketing, and the rest of you are all fired, especially the shrub guy. Now, we've got work to do. Meeting dismissed!"

The advertising department did a great job on bringing Shane to life in a series of newspaper ads, and soon after the meeting, Clive was reading aloud from the morning edition of *The Snudslian* as Velly ate her breakfast and Rennie was trying to feed Mrs. Henderson her horrible Snail 'N' Egg mush discretely under the table.

"Shane the Shrew says: Great leapin' rattlesnakes, kids, it's brand new! Don't get peanut butter — get new LARP! Why it's nicer than a new saddle 'n' stirrups, I plum reckon. Goldern it, just for you buckeroos from all your pardners down home at Nut-Tastic!"

Velly dropped her spoon into her cereal bowl with a loud clank.

"Ulp," she said. "Uh, Rennie, Rennie, uh . . ."

But Rennie was more absorbed in feeding Mrs. Henderson than in listening to what either her father or Velly were saying.

"Oh he's just making it up," she said, without looking up from under the table. "It's just like when I was little, and Snow White went to live in a cottage with the Seven Emergency Rescue Helicopter Pilots."

"No, Rennie," said Velly, "listen . . ."

"Attention! Attention!" Clive continued. *"Come and meet Shane, the big friendly Shrew from Nut-Tastic! He will be in your town soon, with loads and loads of Larp. Be honest, aren't you curious what all the fuss is about? Don't*

be Peanut Butter Proud, be a new Larp Lover!"

"Ulp," said Rennie, suddenly straightening in her chair.

"What on earth is all this about?" cried Clive to no one in particular, as he threw the paper down. "We've been working like mad things to design a 'peanut butter' factory, not a 'Larp' factory. What's the real name of the stuff? No one from the head office told me about this! Is the name being changed? What? I mean —"

Rennie and Velly sat silently in their chairs.

"This will mean delays, delays, delays," cried Clive, getting more flustered and confused. "I thought it was called — holy cats! It's going to cost millions! What are we going to do? Helen! Helen!"

He ran wildly out of the room, calling for his wife in a panicked voice. The two girls looked across the table at one another.

"A shrew," said Rennie softly, "called Shane?"

"Yes," answered Velly.

"A cowboy shrew?"

Velly nodded.

"Yup," she said.

"Good heavens," said Rennie.

It hadn't been more than a few weeks since the girls had started *Operation Larp*, and as far as they knew the only effect had been that lots of children in their part of the country had begun to prefer the name "Larp" to the name "peanut butter". Of course, the mystery had been reported in the local newspapers, but only once or twice, and nothing at all had happened to suggest to Rennie and Velly that their prank would be responsible for something like Shane the Shrew.

"But we only changed a few SPREAD-O labels," whispered Rennie. "What does Nut-Tastic have to do with it? It's a different company altogether."

"I don't know," said Velly, "but according to this, Shane and the Nut-Tastic people will be in Snudsley on Friday, when SPREAD-O will be unveiling your parents' plans for their new factory in Snudsley West."

"What are we going to do?" asked Rennie frantically.

"How should I know?" said Velly, her voice rising. "I'm supposed to be the one that panics —you're supposed to know what we're going to do. So what are we going to do?"

"I don't know what we're going to do!"

At that moment Ken burst into the kitchen, carrying a pile of cardboard protest signs.

"IT'S A DISASTER!" he cried in a shrill voice.

"WE KNOW!" they cried back in similar voices.

Ken seemed to have lost his usual cheerful calm in the face of unfortunate events like this one.

"Oh, you've seen the paper have you?" he said. "What are we going to do?"

"I don't know! I don't know!" said Rennie for about the eighth and ninth time.

"Take a look at this," said Ken, and held out one of the signs for them. It had NO PEANUT BUTTER PIN-HEADS printed on it in black letters.

"Lils and I have been getting things ready for the protest rally that's going to take place at the SPREAD-O presentation this Friday," explained Ken. "Now we discover that we're protesting the wrong thing. It's called 'Larp' now! Ruinous! Tragic!"

"Couldn't you get new signs made up?" asked Velly.

"It's too late now to print new signs before Friday," replied Ken sadly.

He plonked one of the signs on the table, took out a

felt-tip marker, and put a big black scribble through the words 'peanut butter' and scrawled the word 'Larp' above them.

"Does that work? Yes, that will work, I suppose," he said, though he didn't sound very certain. "Anyway, I think we can still get the message across, even with botched signs like these, don't you? No smelly new factories in Snudsley!"

Ken spread all his signs out on the table and was looking at them woefully when Clive came running back into the kitchen.

"Well, it's an *offical* catastrophe," said Clive. "I just got off the phone with the marketing director at SPREAD-O, and they don't quite know — what's going on — but —"

Ken whipped the signs off the table and tried to lean over in front of the others, which were stacked on the floor and against the legs of a chair.

"What's this I see?" said Clive in a breathless voice, reading the signs from behind Ken. "NO PEANUT BUT-TER PINHEADS? FACTOR OUT FACTORIES? SLING SQUEE OUT OF SNUDSLEY?"

"It's not you *personally*, Clive," explained Ken, "you're a peach. You're both peaches, you and Helen I mean. Peaches. Letting us live here and all. But we, as concerned citizens, don't want any more factories in Snudsley . . ."

"As of this moment, there aren't any factories in Snudsley," yelled Clive, "and if this one doesn't get built, there also won't be any Parsleys in Snudsley. And if there aren't any Parsleys, I will give you my personal promise that you won't be able to find any Sprouts either!"

Clive was much smaller than Ken but he could get very angry, and he was very angry now. Ken gulped and collected up his signs hastily.

"They're going," he stammered, "I'll do them in the shed, sorry, Clive. I'll just, in the shed, I'll —" and he ran out the door.

Clive sat down at the table and stared off moodily into space.

"He brought his family into my house," he mumbled to himself, "and he brought a duck. He planted carrots and peas in my bathroom sink. Now he's organizing a protest against my peanut butter factory. I mean Larp factory. I mean — I can't — I can't —"

Velly thought she should try to change the subject.

"Quite a thing," she said quickly, "this Larp thing. Don't you think? Quite a thing . . ."

"Quite a *devastating* thing," said Clive, taking off his

glasses and rubbing his eyes wearily, "if they decide to change the name. The SPREAD-O people are up in arms — even they don't know what that glop made from peanuts is called anymore. It's a complete panic, and we have to cover both the 'peanut butter' and the 'Larp' alternatives."

"Is it really so important, dad?" asked Rennie. "It's just a word, after all, ha ha."

"It's the sign," said Clive. "Your mother had designed a lovely sign in antique chrome for the front, it runs all along the top ridge of the building in letters twenty feet high, saying SPREAD-O PEANUT BUTTER. But if we change it to LARP there will be a lot of extra space and frankly she doesn't know what to do with it. She's back there in the office, trying to make it say SPREAD-O REALLY GREAT LARP, or even SPREAD-O LARP LARP LARP LARP, over and over, but the spacing isn't working out and the poor woman is going crackers."

He looked as though he might start to cry.

Rennie glanced over at Velly, who glanced back at

her. How could have their brilliant and harmless little idea become such an enormous mess?

"Oh well," said Clive, wiping his eyes again, "no good being moody about it. Got to buck up, yes? It will probably all turn out all right; it always does. Helen and I can work it out, somehow, because nothing and nobody can stop this project. Certainly not a bunch of veg-heads with misspelled protest signs!"

"That's right, Mr. Parsley!" said Velly encouragingly.

He moved towards the door, but before he left he turned back at the girls with a courageous smile —

"And so, my dears, as the old saying goes, it's back to the —"

"Drawing board, I suppose?" said Rennie.

"No," said Clive triumphantly, "it's back to the Complementary, Individually Wrapped, Mint-Scented Personal Cleansing Towelette!"

"Well, now's a good time to take a look around and see where we are," said Rennie later that evening when the two girls were alone in their bedroom.

Velly nodded.

"A short while ago we switched the labels on a small number of jars in some local supermarkets, changing the name of their contents from 'peanut butter' to 'Larp'. As a result of this, our parents are now at each other's throats, we are wanted by the local police, and somehow we have created a cartoon cowboy shrew without even meaning to. And to top it all off, the muffin business and the architecture business are both a hair's-breadth from going bankrupt, we will all have to live on the street, and you and I will spend the rest of our lives begging for pennies on street corners while we play zithers or something."

"Zithers . . ." said Velly absently.

Rennie sat on the edge of the bed and let her head fall wearily.

"Honestly, Velly," she sighed, "sometimes I wish you didn't get us into so much trouble."

"*WHAT*?" exclaimed Velly. "I only wrote the story in the newspaper — you're the one who thought it would be a great idea to actually do it!"

"That's because you're always too chicken!" said Rennie angrily. "You never have enough guts to actually do anything, you just sit around and dream!"

"I do not," said Velly, "it's just that sometimes I think about other people instead of myself!"

"I think of other people," argued Rennie, "I always think of you, and how you can't do anything on your own!"

"I have to take care of the duck on my own," said Velly, "and I'm trying to keep our parents happy when we're all under one roof, and all you can suggest are more stupid ways to make it all worse!"

"I wish I could take care of Mrs. Henderson, and help our parents be friends, and be nicer," said Rennie, "but it's no use — every time I think of something kind and sensitive to do, I always end up thinking of how much funnier it would be to pull a great prank."

"Fine! But don't blame me for the mess we're in," said Velly. "I could easily come up with any number of clever pranks to do, cleverer than yours, I just don't want to."

"If I believed that," said Rennie, "I could believe anything — even that I could turn into a nicer and more agreable person."

"Ha!" said Velly.

"Anyway," said Rennie, "I'm totally confused at this point. We ought to sleep on it, and try to figure a way out of this mess in the morning. Good night, Vel."

"Good night," said Velly moodily.

Rennie turned off the light, and the bedroom was plunged into darkness. And silence.

At least for a little while.

"QUACK!" Suddenly Mrs. Henderson began bouncing and flapping up into the bed, and Rennie thrashed herself out from under the covers.

"QUACK QUACK QUACK QUACK —"

"OUT YOU GO!" cried Rennie, and the light went on again. Velly kept her eyes closed, but she could hear Rennie stomping off into the bathroom, and the clucks and splashes of her struggling to put Mrs. Henderson into the bathtub.

I will think of *something, something*, thought Velvet as she began to doze off. I never do anything? I'm really not so nicey-nice as all that. I can think of pranks and hoaxes and tricks and bricks and boxes and pranks and I can be clever ever so never so clever . . .

She was sitting on a wide granite boulder beside a beautiful mountain stream, when a small frog hopped up next to her and opened a copy of *The Snudsley Suggester*.

"You see," she explained, "I'm just as clever as she is, really I am. She just does things without thinking them through, that's all."

"I've heard that," said the frog, not looking up from the paper.

"And she's braver than me," continued Velly. "I usually get nervous at the last moment, and something always goes wrong."

"Tell *me* about it," said the frog, and he folded up his

newspaper and hopped down into the stream.

"I guess I'm just going to have to think of the most *genius* and *brilliant* prank, and then do it," said Velly to a lobster and a slice of strawberry-filled cheesecake, who were both winding pocket watches. "Then she will have different idea about Velvet Sprout. What do you think?"

"That's a wonderful idea, dear," murmured Mrs. Henderson suddenly into her ear. The little duck had just come up and nestled comfortably beside her. "That will make her sit up and take notice. You're your own person aren't you? You're not a little duckling any longer."

"Exactly," said Velly, "and I have my own ideas — terrific ideas. And I can pull them off by myself, too."

"Well, good for you dear," said Mrs. Henderson.

"Huzzah!" cried a number of voices. There were animals in the meadow, along with a lot of strange objects —

teapots and picture frames and clams and birdcages — and everything was chattering and scuttling about, and jumping, and now and then they would all cheer — "Huzzah!" Velly could hear Mrs. Henderson talking to her, but she couldn't understand what she was saying.

"Huzzah!" said the crowd again.

"Mrs. Henderson, can you think of anything?" asked Velly over the shouting. "I mean a brilliant prank? Couldn't you help me out, even if I'm not your mom?"

"Well, as a matter of fact, yes," began Mrs. Henderson. "You see, my idea was —"

But Velly couldn't see or hear her anymore. The crowd of peculiar objects and animals was pressing in on her, and she was trying to run after Mrs. Henderson, but she knew she would never catch her. The little duck was getting farther away, and Velly could barely hear her voice.

"What?" she cried. "What was your idea, Mrs. Henderson?"

"*It was* —"

But then she was awake, in the darkened room in the middle of the night, with only the sounds of Rennie's soft breathing next to her, and Mrs. Henderson's splashing in the bathtub — and in her head, no brilliant idea at all.

Five

Velly did fall back to sleep eventually, and in fact rose later than usual the next morning. Rennie and Mrs. Henderson were gone — already downstairs having breakfast she supposed — so she got out of bed and began to get dressed in order to join them.

And as she was trying to remember her dream, suddenly — as will often happen first thing in the morning — something popped from out of nowhere into her empty head. It was *the idea*; a wonderful, brilliant, genius, excellent, superb, exceptional, overall honey-of-an-idea that would not only get back at Mr. Box for closing down *The Snudsley Suggester*, but also impress Rennie with her cleverness and prankiness and bravery. And the only thing she needed was an egg.

"Velly! Help help help!"

It was Rennie's voice, calling from the kitchen. Velly finished dressing quickly and ran to see what was the matter.

When she got to the kitchen she found Rennie backed helplessly into a corner, next to the basin, while on the countertop Mrs. Henderson hopped and quacked and flapped at her in the grip of some kind of ferocious frenzy.

"QUACK QUACK QUACK QUACK!" screamed Mrs. Henderson.

"What on earth?" said Velly as she gathered up the ecstatic duck, plunged her into the wicker hatbox, and closed the lid. Rennie put her hand to her chest and drooped with visible relief.

"Oh thank goodness, you came at last!"

"What for heaven's sake happened?" asked Velly.

"She wanted breakfast, but we were out of boiled eggs and slugs," explained Rennie, a bit out of breath, "so I started to feed her with crackers dipped into Ken's Eggplant Crème, and she went completely nuts! She cracked up! She flipped her little feathery wig!"

"She liked it?" grinned Velly.

"Liked it? I thought she was going to rip my arm out of its socket! Don't *ever* feed her any of that stuff, whatever you do. Don't let her smell it even!"

"Well, she's calming down now," said Velly, and indeed the quacks that had been proceeding from the closed hatbox were getting softer. "I guess we ought to go out and buy some more eggs, don't you agree?"

"A lot more," said Rennie, still a bit shaken. "Let's go right away, before anyone gets hurt."

"We can get some slugs from the banks of the Drip on our way back," said Velly.

It was a beautiful day as they walked to the supermarket, with Velly humming and grinning.

"I'm sorry about last night, Velly" asked Rennie, "but what are you so cheerful about? I thought you always worried about things going wrong. And they are going wrong, they really really are."

"Oh I don't know," smiled Velly, "sometimes things work out all right by themselves, don't they? Anyway, I just have a feeling that our troubles will soon be over."

"That's right," said Rennie, "we'll laugh about all this soon enough, when our troubles are over."

But, I'm sorry to say, their troubles were far from over.

Now, speaking of troubles, I hope that I haven't given any of you the impression that Principal Box had been idle all this time — that he had been sitting happily in his office chair, looking over reports of the teachers' salaries and reading long, dull letters from the PTA about playground equipment, like a normal school principal. Far from it.

Ever since he had tried to trick the girls into squealing on one another his brain had scarcely ever stopped whirring and zizzing in his skull, trying to figure out a foolproof way to get the goods on Rennie and Velly, so that he could have them expelled from the school forever. Now that *The Snudsley Suggester* was a thing of the past, he was sure they would soon be up to something even more sinister. If only he knew what exactly . . .

He tried following them around the school, but within its halls they were always as good as gold — doing their chemistry experiments, conjugating *jouer* and reading up on the history of the Alaska Gold Rush. They were the perfect students; they were *maddeningly* perfect. And it was infuriating, because he was *sure* that they had to be up to something, they just *had* to be!

And then one day he noticed, as he was spying on them from around the corner, that they were frequently followed by a little girl as they left the school. A young girl, too young to be in school, who always carried two strange objects in her hands. Perhaps he could contact that little girl in some way. But how?

You can imagine his gleeful surprise, then, when he stumbled over the selfsame little girl one afternoon, waiting for Rennie and Velly under the Snudsley Oak, and having an intense conversation with her two strange objects.

"They don't mean it, they live somewhere else," she was saying in a growly voice, wiggling one of the things. "Yes they do, and they mean it," she replied in a squeaky voice, and wiggled the other.

"Hello, little girl," said the Principal oilily, "and what's your little name?"

"I'm Abigail Braintree," said Abigail eagerly. "I'm four and three-quarters years old! And I have two dolls here named Soapy and Rumba!"

"Well, that *is* interesting!" grinned the Principal. "Tell me, are you friends with the Sprout girl and Parsley?"

"I know Rennie and Velly! They are my very very best friends!" said Abigail.

"Good, good," said the Principal. And though it bruised his dignity somewhat, he sat down next to her at the base of the Snudsley Oak, and tried to put on a casual and friendly air.

"Do you know, Abigail," he said softly, "just *exactly* what they are up to, these days?"

There was a flurry of wiggling from Rumba and Soapy, and some yips and growls from Abigail.

"Rumba says they are up to something new, but Soapy says he doesn't know what it is."

"How can we find out, do you think, Abigail?" said the Principal gently and nauseatingly. "Can you find out and perhaps inform me as to their activities?"

"You talk funny, mustache-man," said Abigail. "Anyway mommy says I can't walk with them any more, 'cause they live in Rennie's house and it's too far now."

"But you will be at the Presentation on Friday, won't you?" asked the Principal. "The SPREAD-O Presentation? You and your mommy and daddy will be there, I'm sure."

"Uh huh. I like SPREAD-O best, it goes with strawsberry and rapsberry and and not goes with —"

"Could you try to listen," interrupted Mr. Box, "and then tell me what they say?"

"What do I get?" asked Abigail abruptly.

"Well, what do you want?" he asked, taken aback but with a simpering grin. "Would you like a new dolly?"

"No, I want twenty bucks," said Abigail.

"Twenty," gulped the Principal . . .

"Bucks," he gulped again . . . and then glued the phony

smile once more to his face, and spoke in gentle tones.

"All right, little girl Abigail," he said at last, "if you let me know what horrid things those two girls are doing, you can have twenty dollars all to yourself. Twenty whole dollars! My! What will you do with all that money?"

Abigail held up Rumba and Soapy alternately.

"Legs," she said. "Eyes."

That same afternoon, in his office, Mr. Whacker sat fidgeting in his chair and drumming his fingers on the desk. Suddenly he heard the voice of Miss Limb through 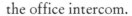 the office intercom.

"Squee the Squirr—I mean, Mr. Trevellyn is here to see you, sir," she said.

"All right," sighed Mr. Whacker. "Send him in."

Llewellyn Trevellyn entered the office and assumed, very dramatically as usual, a fine heroic stance in front of Mr. Whacker's desk.

"Alas," he cried out, "for I am all undone!"

"What's the matter with you now?" growled Mr. Whacker.

"It's the children, and the Larp" sniffed Mr. Trevellyn. "Larp here, Larp there, Larp all around the town. In every venue at which I am privileged to appear, the children ask only for Larp. When I offer them the free samples of our fine product, they cry out as if in a single voice — 'A pox on your peanut butter, Squee, for we shall have Larp, and Larp alone!' I tell you I am *decidedly* frantic."

"Yes," agreed Mr. Whacker, "I know all about it already, so shut up. Now listen, Trevellyn, I want to get to the bottom of this once and for all, and so I have a special job for you."

"Pray continue."

"This coming Friday," said Mr. Whacker, "we are holding an event in Snudsley, at which we will announce the plans for the new factory being built in the town. All the press will be there, I will be there, and of course you will be there as well."

"Go on, go on, Weed," said Mr. Trevellyn. "May I call you Weed?"

"No you may not!" said Mr. Whacker.

"Anyway it's pronounced 'Wade'. My parents were from Sweden."

"Really?" asked Mr. Trevellyn. "Whereabouts? Stockholm? Gothenburg? Lund?"

"Iowa, actually," said Mr. Whacker, turning slightly pink. "Sweden, in Iowa. Little town outside Boone. "

"I comprehend all," said Mr. Trevellyn. "In any and all eventualities, I do pray you continue. I am *unreservedly* attentive."

"Will you stop talking like that?" shouted Mr. Whacker. "You're going to drive me bats, you hambone! Now I want you, on that day, to circulate through the crowd in your Squee suit, and see if you don't overhear something which might explain this Larp business. I'm pretty sure that some people from Nut-Tastic will be there, and I am *completely* sure that they will be plotting to do something that will disrupt the Presentation, destroy my reputation, and reduce the SPREAD-O Peanut Butter Company to atoms. We've got to find out what they are doing, and stop it!"

"I see," said Mr. Trevellyn. "Well, sir, you may rest assured of my absolute cooperation."

"Good," said Mr. Whacker. "This company has made peanut butter for many years, and will continue to do so, in spite of this fiasco. I promise you — after this Friday, the word 'Larp' will be completely forgotten — as completely forgotten as your acting career!"

Meanwhile, in *his* office, Mr. Tode sat looking at a large grinning shrew with beach ball eyes that stood before his desk. Miss Snip was also there, looking rather smug.

"So this," he smiled, "is the famous Shane, eh? Splendid. Shane the Shrew. Marvelous. Super, really super."

"Thank you, Mr. Tode," said Miss Snip.

"And he is ready to appear in Snudsley this Friday? The costume is complete, perfect, all set? No problems, no trouble, no mistakes?"

"Not that we know of, sir," said Miss Snip. "We've tried him out with some test groups, and everything seems to work. His eyes blink, his arms move, his head stays on."

"Oh well that *is* reassuring, certainly," said Mr. Tode. "I mean at the absolute *minimum* his head should stay on. By the way . . ."

"Yes, sir?"

"Well, I *am* rather curious — who have we got in there? May I take a peek?"

"Oh certainly, sir," said Miss Snip, and she lifted the giant shrew head off of the giant shrew body, and revealed the face of a rather sleepy looking young man with shaggy blond hair.

"Mr. Tode," said Miss Snip, "this is Woody."

"Dude," said Woody.

Mr. Tode's renowned smile fell quickly from his face.

"I thought he was supposed to talk cowboy," he said testily. "Can he do cowboy?"

"Can I do cowboy what?" asked Woody.

"Woody's from the mailroom, Mr. Tode," said Miss Snip quickly. "He's only been with us for a week, and no one else would volunteer. He shouldn't have to speak too much while in the costume, so I'm sure it will be all right."

"Silence is golden, dude," agreed Woody.

"Well, I hope you know your business," said Mr. Tode, his smile reappearing. "Because we want this Friday to be a complete success, young man. We want everyone who thinks of the word 'Larp' to think, not of SPREAD-O, but of Shane the Shrew and his friends at Nut-Tastic. It will be your job to go among the people at the Presentation, giving out free samples and being as jolly as you can manage. Make sure everyone sees you, gets a sample, and remembers the company name. Think you can do it?"

"If I don't run into anything," said Woody. "This head is *totally* hard to see out of . . ."

Six

So the fatal Friday came at last — the day of the SPREAD-O Factory Presentation, which was taking place in the public square at the end of Main Street, under the greeny-bronzey feet of General Cuthbert Snudsley's statue. The new factory meant quite a lot to the whole town, and everyone was going to be in attendance.

There was a sense of excitement at the breakfast table of the Parsley's house that morning, with Sprouts and Parsleys bustling about, and Rennie and Velly whispering together at one end.

"I want us to get into the supermarket this morning," said Rennie, "and switch a few more SPREAD-O labels before the Presentation begins."

"What for?" asked Velly.

"It will be fun, for one thing, if we can get away with it," grinned Rennie. "Just imagine — everyone looking for us, the zany Larp hoaxers, and us changing labels right under their very noses."

"So then we can get caught and confess and blame it all on Mr. Box?" asked Velly hopefully.

"I'm not interested in getting caught anymore," said Rennie. "I've definitely decided that this whole prank has been more fun than several barrels of monkeys stacked on top of one another. I plan on doing a lot more."

Velly chewed her omelet thoughtfully, and considered her own brilliant plan. If it could work out, Rennie would be so impressed with her cleverness that she would burst. She *had* to pull it off, she simply *had* to.

"Lovely breakfast, Mrs. Sprout," said Rennie.

Lily was beside the stove, making duck egg omelets for everyone, while Clive and Helen were busy loading all the materials for the SPREAD-O Presentation — models, paintings, charts and easels — into the back of their car. In fact they were so busy that for a long time they didn't see Ken standing beside them.

"Ahem," he sort of coughed.

"Yes, Ken?" said Clive without looking up.

"Well," said Ken sheepishly, "it's a bit embarrassing, but I wonder if Lils and I might get a lift to the Presentation from you? I've tried to start up the van but there seems to be something wrong with it."

"Don't see why not," said Clive, folding an easel and a chair and sliding them in.

"Oh terrific, thanks" said Ken hurriedly, and began to load his stack of protest signs into the back of the Parsleys' station wagon.

At last Clive looked up.

"What — what are you doing?" he breathed. His voice was so quiet you could barely hear it.

"Can't carry them all," explained Ken hurriedly, "there's a heck of a lot of them. Plenty of people turning up, you know, for the protest . . ."

Clive tried to stammer out more objections, but he didn't seem to be able to finish a proper sentence.

"But I — how can you — I've never in my — what in the —"

"Thanks a lot, Clive, you're a peach really really a peach," said Ken, and he finished loading the last signs before he dashed back into the house.

"Again with the peaches," fumed Clive. "I don't want to be a peach . . ."

"Now now, Clive," said Helen soothingly, "they're our guests after all. And it's certain that the protesters will be there, whether we give them a lift or not."

"You're right, dear," sighed Clive, glancing with despair at a sign reading NUTS TO PEANUTS. "I suppose there's nothing to do but grin and bear it. Besides which, we have considerably bigger fish to fry today — if all goes well, this evening will see *Parsley & Parsley* back on the tippy-top of the architecture game!"

"Oh, that would be lovely," said Helen.

After packing in all the protest signs, Ken slid into the kitchen, whistling a merry air and clapping Lily cheerfully on the back.

"Well, I got us a lift into town," he said.

"Lovely, dear," said Lily as she slid another omelet onto Rennie's plate. "Who's taking us in, exactly?"

"You just wait and see, Lils, old girl," said Ken.

"Thanks again for the lovely breakfast, Mrs. S," said Rennie after her last mouthful, "we'd better get going now."

And then, as the two girls rose and began to get ready to leave, Velly suddenly turned to Lily and whispered —

"Mom can I have a duck egg?"

"Sorry, hon, I just used the last one," said Lily. "What on earth do you want it for?"

"Oh nothing," said Velly, a crestfallen look on her face. "I just thought — I don't know — if you had a spare one —"

"Come on, Vel," said Rennie from the front door, "time's-a-wasting!"

Not having a duck egg when you have a genius plan for one might seem terribly unlucky, but actually that was a stroke of enormous good fortune compared with the rest of the morning's events, which went spectacularly badly.

And that was because Abigail Braintree wanted a package of chocolate cookies to eat during the Presentation, and she dragged her mother into the supermarket to buy them. And the cookies that she wanted just happened to be located in the Bakery aisle, around the corner from Jam, Jelly and Marmalade, and directly next to Peanut Butter.

And even that wasn't the really spectacularly bad thing. The really horribly bad and fabulously unfortunate thing was — that was precisely the spot where

Velly and Rennie were standing at the moment Abigail
walked up, quietly changing thirty jars of SPREAD-O
peanut butter into Larp.

"Hi, Velly," said Abigail when she saw them. "Hi, Rennie. I've got chocolate cookies. They're chocolate. What are
you doing?"

At first, neither girl could bear to look down — but
they knew they would eventually have to. And they did, and
there she was; little Abigail, clutching Rumba and Soapy
and a crumpled, slobbery box of cookies, gazing up at them
with a wide smile.

"Oh, nothing," said Rennie.

"It's *something*," said Abigail in what she thought was a
scolding, grown-up voice. "I can see you're doing *something*."

"It's nothing, Abigail," hissed Velly, "so now please
please go away."

"This is the SPREAD-O section," said Abigail in a
far-too-loud voice. "I like SPREAD-O. You're doing something to the SPREAD-O jars. What are you doing to the
SPREAD-O jars?"

And then, at long last, a light
dawned within her tiny head.

"IT'S YOU!" she screamed
gleefully, dropping everything in
her arms onto the ground. "LARP
LARP! YOU'RE DOING IT!"

"SHHHHHHH!" hissed both the girls together.

They crammed the remaining jars of Larp or peanut butter (it didn't matter which was which at that point) back onto the shelves, grabbed up all their equipment, jumped over Abigail and made for the door as fast as they could — but not fast enough, I'm afraid.

Because at that moment Mr. Cling, the manager of the supermarket, came around the corner to investigate.

"What a lot of noise —" he began, and that's when he saw exactly what it was that Velly and Rennie were up to, and quickly put two and two together. To say that Mr. Cling looked surprised would mean a brand new definition of the word "surprised" in the dictionary —

SURPRISED (adj.): State with the face turning green, lips twisted like corkscrews, and eyes shooting out on stalks. Frequently accompanied with hair standing up like bamboo shoots.

He looked like that and more — the dictionary doesn't mention it but I'd also like to add that it appeared as though poodles might start leaping out of his ears at any moment.

"IT'S IT'S IT'S YOU YOU YOU!" he shouted.

"Time to go?" asked Velly.

"Oh I think so," said Rennie.

The girls dropped everything and ran as fast as they could down to the other end of the aisle — but once again, they hadn't reckoned on Kevin, the sad Sun-Squirt Acorn.

"Hi, I'm Kevin, the sad Sun-UUUUNGH—!" said Kevin as the two girls careened into him and knocked him completely over, flinging little cups of orange juice high into the air and all over the floor. Helpless, they tried to untangle themselves from each other and from Kevin's flailing legs, but they weren't quick enough, and very soon felt two strong hands lifting them high into the air like empty paper shopping bags. Mr. Cling, who held both of them up before his face, grinned horribly.

"Well, my dears," he said, "this is the end of the trail for you two. The jig is up! And the score is *Supermarket Managers: two — Larp Felons: zero!*"

The two girls hung in mid-air like limp puppets and looked nervously at one another, while Mr. Cling began to laugh — not like people actually laugh, but the way the villain used to laugh in old movies:

"Mwah-hah-hah-ha!" he said.

Then he put them down and jerked them roughly towards the door, towards the line of policemen gathering outside for the Presentation, which was due to begin in a few hours.

"Oh well," whispered Velly, "I suppose it had to happen, sooner or later."

"Terrific fun, though," said Rennie.

"I suppose," said Velly. "Guess I'd better get busy with our confession."

And as they were pushed out of the store, behind them, very faintly, they could just hear the voice of Kevin.

"Um, could someone help me up, please?"

❖   ❖   ❖   ❖   ❖

"The police," smiled Mr. Box, leaning back in his office chair with the tips of his fingers pressed together, "are far too busy with the Presentation this afternoon, to deal with the likes of you two." He glanced at the girls who sat again on little chairs before him, and smiled.

"You see," he said, "the police chief told me that it would be inconvenient to expose the two of you as the Larp criminals until after the Presentation is over. The program has been carefully worked out, and they don't want any changes at this point, so they tell me.

"They have asked me if I would mind keeping you locked up here in the school until after it is over, at which time they will be able to deal with you properly. 'Delighted,' I told them, 'delighted. Only *too* delighted!'."

And so there they were, back in the Principal's office, taking their punishment for another prank, and by this time it had started to dawn on Rennie and Velly just how completely out of hand things had become.

"Everyone will be there," continued the Principal, "the Mayor, myself, all the representatives of SPREAD-O, all your fellow students and fellow citizens, and of course all four of your parents. Everyone, in fact — except you."

Mr. Box seemed to think this was very funny, and he chuckled privately to himself, so that his mustache wobbled vaguely on his upper lip.

"Sorry — I was just thinking how lovely it would be if you *could* be there," he giggled. "I mean in a cage, or tied to a pole, or something like that. Think of it. The Larp Wrongdoers apprehended, and publicly humiliated at the new SPREAD-O Factory Presentation. People could throw tomatoes or something. Rotten tomatoes. Quite fitting, I think. Quite *appropriate*."

The two girls gulped.

"Ah well, such ideas are out of fashion," he sighed, and got up out of his chair. "Some people think they are vulgar and cruel."

He put on his coat and took out of his pocket a bunch of keys, which he began to twirl lazily around his forefinger.

"Though not me, I can tell you," he added.

Gingerly, he pulled the two of them out of their chairs by the collars of their shirts, as if they were particularly smelly bits of garbage. He pushed them out his office door and down the corridor of the school towards the empty classroom that was once their newspaper office.

"No, the new view is to be moderate," he continued, "and to try to rehabilitate you two little mad people. All a waste of time, but what can I do? I can only try to keep you out of harm's way — I mean other people's harm's way — until the police can come, and take you away to I-don't-want-to-know-where. Hopefully their methods in that place will prove more *successful* than ours here at the school."

He pushed the two of them into the classroom and closed the door. They heard the lock *click* forcibly, and the Principal chuckle again.

"A pathetic end," they heard his voice say, "to a short, shabby career in crime. I simply knew you were up to no good, and it's very gratifying that you have been captured at last. And now, not only will you be expelled, but you're going up the river with a noticeable, shall we say, lack of paddle! Delicious!"

Rennie and Velly tried the door handle, but it was really very locked. Mr. Box waved at them through the glass.

"I'd love to say 'See you again soon' but I probably won't. I don't get down to the prison very often."

He laughed again and they heard the sound of his footsteps fading away down the hall. Rennie and Velly sat there a long time in silence before either of them said anything. Then Velly spoke.

"We're sunk," she said.

Rennie got up without a word and began walking around the room, collecting chairs and pushing them against a wall, while Velly mumbled dejectedly and stared off into space.

"It's over," she said slowly, "finished. Through. Over and done with. We're washed up, we're in the soup. Deeply in the soup, up to our eyes in soup. Sticky soup. It's the end of the road, the last highway. We're riding off into the

sunset, you and I, and there's this soup, we're sunk up to our eyeballs in this soup, and we're riding down the last highway into the sunset, on *horses* and the *horses* are sticky too with the soup —"

"We got caught all right," said Rennie from her spot by the window, "if that's what you mean."

"Well, it's Confession Time," said Velly brightly. She grabbed a piece of paper and began to speak out loud as she wrote.

"*Now that we are in the soup,*" she said, "*everyone should know that it's all, all the Principal's fault, not ours, we're not guilty, it's all his awful fault, it really is, he is really the one in the soup, it was all him, not us, the soup —*"

"For heaven's sake," shouted Rennie, "will you please *shut up* about the soup and do something to *help* me?"

She was halfway up the wall, on a sort of ladder she had made of stacked-up chairs.

"What — what are you doing?" asked Velly.

"I'm getting us out of here," said Rennie. "Hand me a few more chairs, will you, and I can reach the latch."

"You mean we're going to 'make a break for it'?" asked Velly excitedly.

"Velly," said Rennie, trying to stay calm,

"this is an ordinary schoolroom in Snudsley, not a maximum-security cell in Alcatraz. All we have to do is open these windows from the top and we can climb out and jump down onto the street. The reason for the chairs, see?"

"Wow!" exclaimed Velly. She wadded up her confession, tossed in the wastebasket, and started handing chairs up to Rennie.

And it worked — soon they had climbed out the window and were walking together down the street towards the center of town.

"That sounded like a really great confession, Vel," said Rennie with a hint of sarcasm, but Velly didn't answer. She was a bit distracted because, now that they were free from the Principal's makeshift jail, she started thinking again of her brilliant plan, and with every step towards Main Street a thought echoed through her mind —

What'll I do? was the thought. *What shall I do? What will I do?*

In the distance they could just see a large crowd starting to gather in the square, along with loads of colorful tents and podiums and strings of banners and tables that had been set up for the big SPREAD-O Factory Presentation. But all Velly could think of was eggs.

There's no egg, thought Velly sadly. *No egg. What am I going to do?*

She had her brilliant idea, as you remember, after she

woke up and was watching her mother crack eggs to make duck egg omelets. Duck eggs, you see, are not only bigger than chicken eggs, but they are also thicker and gooier.

So what if she took one of these thick, gloopy eggs with her to the Presentation, and snuck up behind the Principal's chair as he was standing up applauding some speech the Mayor or somebody was making, and placed the egg on his chair directly under his fat bottom?

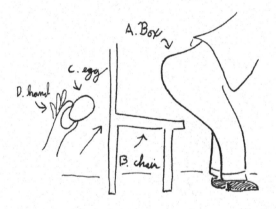

It would be lovely.

He would sit on it, and scream, and turn beet red (as usual), and chaos would follow, with old Boxy being more embarrassed and humiliated than it was possible for human beings to imagine. And it would do so much to impress Rennie — she would admire Velly's daring and prankiness.

It must be said that Velly's idea was perhaps not the cleverest in the world — in fact, if she had had time to reflect on it, she probably would have thought it was kind of lame. But she didn't have time to reflect on it. Time was slipping away. Lily had used all the eggs for breakfast, and Velly was left empty handed. Where could she get a duck egg on such short notice? She certainly couldn't go anywhere near the supermarket, and they wouldn't have duck eggs anyway.

So she thought and thought and thought some more.

"My guess is," Rennie was saying as they walked along, "that SPREAD-O has been in a complete lather over this whole Larp thing and they think it's some kind of sabotage against their company. Since they suspected that, it would never occur to them it's just two girls like us, doing it for no reason at all except to see what would happen."

No eggs no eggs no eggs.

And then, as Rennie went on talking, like a lightening bolt the obvious solution popped into Velly's brain.

Mrs. Henderson!

"And that's probably why we kept on getting away with it," continued Rennie.

Of course! Mrs. Henderson was a duck! It was a gamble, of course, but if Velly could just dash home, and check Mrs. Henderson's hatbox, she might get lucky and find an egg. If only she could be quick enough . . .

Her house was just around the corner. There was no time to lose.

"I have to go!" Velly blurted out.

"What for?" asked Rennie.

"I have to go back home for a minute," said Velly hurriedly "to change my shirt."

"What's wrong with your shirt?"

"It — it isn't changed. BYE!"

Rennie looked at her suspiciously.

"You're not running back so you can blurt out your confession to the Principal, are you?" she asked.

"Of course I'm not."

"Because you snitched on us once before, you know," said Rennie.

"I did not!" exclaimed Velly. "You only thought I did!"

"Oh . . . that's right," said Rennie. "Well, in that case I'll come along with you then."

"NO!" said Velly in a panic. "No, I — I have to change it on my own."

"Your shirt?"

"It's just something I have to do. And I have to do it on my own. I'll catch up with you in a minute, I swear!"

"Um, okay . . ." said Rennie.

Velly dashed down the street and, through the front door of the house, and into the kitchen. Mrs. Henderson's hatbox was in its usual place in the corner next to the back door. She opened it hastily.

"Quack?" inquired Mrs. Henderson sleepily.

Mrs. Henderson was there, but no eggs. At first Velly was discouraged at this, but she was thinking very clearly now, and she knew what to do. She slammed the lid down, picked up the box, and ran back out through the front door.

"Quack," protested Mrs. Henderson.

❖ ❖ ❖ ❖ ❖

As he walked to the Presentation, another idea had begun to percolate in the brain of Principal Box. While the police didn't intend to expose Rennie and Velly as the Notorious Larpsters at the Presentation, there was nothing to stop *him* from letting the cat out of the bag. Oh sure, they were locked up safely in that schoolroom and headed for jail, but there could be no *public humiliation* unless he fingered the two of them in front of the entire town. And that was something he longed for deeply.

"It will be perfect," he told himself. "I'm scheduled to make a speech, one or two people after this Whacker peanut butter guy. I'll just stand up, bow, and inform the good populace of the guilt of the Parsley-Sprout gang, and that I personally have locked them safely up — applause applause applause — and that's where the rotten tomatoes will come in."

He giggled gleefully a moment, and then stopped in his tracks.

"Wait a minute — no one can throw rotten tomatoes at them when they're locked up back in the school! What crummy luck!"

Frantically he tried to think of what to do. He couldn't go back there and fetch them himself; he would be sure to be late. And there was no one else he knew whom he could trust to do it for him.

"I'll find someone," he told himself, "a policeman or something, at the Presentation. I'll ask somebody responsible to go back and get the two little creeps. And after that — *the just rewards!*"

He smirked, and hurried along to the Presentation.

At this same moment, Renate Parsley was also walking alone down the street to the SPREAD-O Presentation, and she was also deeply lost in thought.

Outwardly, she may have looked like a picture of calm and poise, but inside she was seething again — but this time she was seething with worry and confusion. For the first time in her life, one of her pranks had had much more of an effect than she had intended, instead of much less. She should have been happy with this, but it had had so many unforeseen consequences for her, that she just didn't know how to deal with it at all.

First there was her family — they were fighting with the Sprouts because of her — she was the one who had suggested that they live together.

And now *Operation Larp* had gotten so out of hand that Rennie actually didn't know what was happening anymore, and she didn't know what to do to stop it. Or if she even *should* stop it.

"It's all gone wrong," she mumbled. "What to do? What to do? I never meant it. Velly and Mrs. Henderson and Larp, and mom and dad, and the Sprouts — it's all a terrible mess, and it was just supposed to be a joke, just a joke."

She walked faster, but it only made her feel worse.

"Mom and dad! They're going to lose their business, and it's all my fault. All because of that stupid Larp — got to do something, got to think of something!"

No one else could see it happen, but at that moment a little Rennie in a white gown and with a peaceful expression appeared next to her shoulder.

"Why don't you try to make a truce between your parents and the Sprouts, my dear?" asked White Rennie. "You could give your parents a present, and say it came from the Sprouts, and then all would be forgiven."

"That would be a start," agreed Rennie. "That's a good idea."

But at that moment another Rennie, in a red dress and with a nasty smirk on her face, appeared on her other shoulder.

"How will that solve anything?" the Red Rennie snarled. "That's going to save your parents' business? That's going to get you out of trouble with the police, and with school? Oh, PLEASE! Better to try to wreak some more havoc and chaos at the Presentation. What you need now is a deluxe and amazing full-color Colossal Prank!"

"Yes," said Rennie, with a grin, "that's right! And after all, I have to get back at the Principal — I promised Velly I would come up with an idea."

"That's a good girl," giggled Red Rennie.

"No," exclaimed White Rennie, "don't you see? Jokes and pranks are what started all the trouble! You must try to show your Good Intentions, and everything will come out right."

"That's right," apologized Rennie, "I agree. I'm sorry. You're right. Good Intentions, that's right."

"Good Intentions, *Schmood Intentions*," exclaimed Red Rennie. "You can't eat Good Intentions, and what are you going to do when your parents have no money? Better to *destroy* Larp in a ball of *flames*, and wreak horrible revenge on the Principal into the bargain. Ha ha ha haha!"

"No no, it isn't right," shouted White Rennie "she must change her wicked ways!"

"Shut up!" said Red Rennie. "She's good at pranks, they've always worked perfectly for her up until now!"

"Excuse me . . ." said Rennie.

"That's the point — they don't work any more! They're toxic! They're nothing but big big big trouble! *This is no time for pranks!*"

"Forget it! *There was never a better time for pranks!*"

"EXCUSE ME!" said Rennie again.

"What is it?" asked Red and White Rennie together.

"We're here," said Rennie, "at the SPREAD-O Presentation."

If Rennie's brain was all muddled, she fit in perfectly with the scene on Snudsley's Main Street. The area in front of the supermarket was crowded with people, and they had erected a large and colorful podium across the statue

of General Cuthbert at one end of the street. There were colored streamers hanging from the streetlights and the trees, and various tables and chairs had been set up along the pavement.

There were also quite a few policemen here and there, mostly just to keep the crowds in order and out of the way of the officials in charge of the Presentation.

As Rennie drew closer she saw that the Principal had been right, everyone important in Snudsley was there. She spotted the Mayor, Mr. Box himself, Mr. Cling and several other businessy-looking men and women standing and chatting on the podium. On one side of the podium she saw her own parents, still fussing over their easel loaded with charts and diagrams. They even had a little model of the new factory in a glass box, all made of cardboard and toothpicks and bits of sponge.

A bit further down the street from the podium were Velly's mom and dad, at the center of a large group of anti-SPREAD-O protesters. They were all carrying signs, which said things like LARP IS LOOPY, and NO SQUIRRELS FOR SNUDSLEY. Lily and Ken had put up a table with their muffins and several of Ken's new spreads set out upon it, and the unlucky few who had tried to taste some of these had faces which bore expressions that were, in a word, inexpressible.

"Hi, Mr. Sprout," said Rennie, "Mrs. Sprout. You brought some of the new Veg-Spreads, I see."

"Sure," said Ken with a broad smile. "I decided it would be a nice thing to provide refreshments for all the protesters."

Several people were standing close by, holding their

protest signs, and looking at Ken's muffin-and-spread display with expressions of faint horror.

"Suppose people don't like them?" asked Rennie.

"They're free," answered Ken.

"Look," said Lily, pointing at a strange-looking animal up on the podium, "isn't that Squee the Squirrel?"

"It must be," said Rennie.

Of course, everyone knew Squee the Squirrel, he was almost as famous as the President of the United States.

"From watching the SPREAD-O commercials," said Rennie, "I always thought he was a four-inch-high lump of animated putty. But there he is, as big as life."

"But . . . if that's Squee," said Lily, looking over Rennie's shoulder, "who in the world is this?"

Rennie spun around and saw another large furry animal moving towards them through the crowd, a big blue pouch hanging from his neck by a strap. Without a sound he pushed up to the Sprouts' refreshment table and handed

Rennie and Lily two little jars with labels reading 'New Nut-Tastic Larp'.

"It must be Shane," whispered Rennie.

"Yes," said Lily.

They hadn't taken the samples, and Shane tried again to shove them into their hands. Finally he spoke in a muffled voice —

"Take it, it's Larp."

"What?"

"Dude, it's Larp," said Shane in an exasperated voice. "I mean — *goldern it, buckaroos, it's Larp for ya, yippee kiyiyaay!* Now take it, lady — I gotta keep moving or I'm going to get fired."

"Okay . . ."

Timidly, Lily took the Larp, and Shane moved back into the crowd, handing out more samples right and left.

Seven

Up on the podium, lots of people were gathering, including Mr. Whacker and Miss Limb, who were talking with the Mayor and the Principal.

The Mayor was a round and jolly-looking gentleman, who was always smiling and nodding. Of course you already know what Mr. Whacker looks like — he was trying to smile but looked sweaty and uncomfortable as usual. Miss Limb stood next to him, clutching a clipboard and a lot of papers. And the Principal stood behind them all, mumbling to himself and glancing around nervously.

And behind *him*, just underneath the podium, in the shadows and completely out of sight, was Velly.

"Please, Mrs. Henderson," pleaded Velly to the closed hatbox on her lap, "would you please give me an egg? Just a little one? I really need it."

"Quack." said Mrs. Henderson.

"Please? Pretty please?"

"Quack quack."

"Listen, you — you *duck*," she whispered harshly, "you'd better lay an egg right this moment or I promise you that you'll be swimming in a tureen of orange sauce by suppertime. Now get with it!"

"Quack."

Velly sighed and looked around. She had found the perfect place, right under the Principal's chair, which was set rather towards the back of the podium. The podium was entirely open at the back, and she knew that when the speeches started the Principal would stand up and applaud, and then sit down again, and then stand up and applaud again, and then sit down, and so on. It would be so easy to slip her hand up and put an egg on the seat of that chair, so very easy, and funny, and brave — if only she had an egg!

"Mrs. Henderson, hurry up," she said desperately.

"Quack," replied Mrs. Henderson.

"Well well well," said a gruff voice. Velly's heart stopped as she looked up from the hatbox to see a policeman bending over her.

"You can't sit under here, miss. It's guests only behind here," he said. "And by the way, what's in there, anyway?" he asked, pointing his nightstick at Mrs. Henderson's box.

"A hat," gulped Velly, scrambling out from under the podium, "I thought it might rain, you see. That's why I was crouched under here, in fact."

"Well, it's unlikely to rain, miss, seeing as it's a lovely day."

"Yes," said Velly, "silly me. It *is* lovely, isn't it?"

"Added to which, I couldn't help but notice, miss," said the policeman severely, "that your 'hat' said '*quack*' a minute ago."

"Oh did I say 'hat'?" stammered Velly. "I meant 'duck'. I brought a duck with me. Nothing special, just a common old duck, you know."

"A duck? Why would you bring a duck with you?"

"In case it might . . . it might . . . rain . . ."

"Very well," said the policeman, drawing himself up.

"There's no law against carrying a duck around in a hatbox, though perhaps there ought to be. But you still have to leave this area. And don't come back, Miss, I've got my eye on you."

"Yes, sir," said Velly, and she crawled around to the side of the podium and melted into the crowd. She felt cowardly again — she wasn't used to being confronted by policemen.

"Whew, that was close, Mrs. Henderson," she said. "I've never been so scared in my life!"

But Mrs. Henderson didn't go "Quack", which was peculiar.

"Mrs. Henderson?" said Velly softly.

"Mrs. Henderson?" she said again, and cautiously opened the lid of the box.

There, inside the box, next to a very contented-looking Mrs. Henderson, was a lovely large cream-colored egg.

"Brilliant! Good job, Mrs. Henderson!" exclaimed Velly.

This was it. It would work now. She was excited, and felt her stomach start to flip up and down again, but she knew just what she had to do. She knew that, armed with her egg, she could be brave enough. The policeman had moved away to the other side of the street and was talking to some ladies further on. With great care Velly closed the lid of the hatbox, and began to gently creep, alone and unseen, back to her perfect spot under the podium.

But Velly wasn't to remain alone and unseen for long, because unfortunately her hiding place was soon discovered. There was a presence — a familiar squeaking, a familiar grunting, and then a familiar four and three-quarter year old human voice speaking to her.

"Hi Velly," said Abigail. "Is Mrs. Henderson in the box? Does Mrs. Henderson like to be in the box? Rumba puts Soapy in a box sometimes but Soapy doesn't like it and comes right out. Can I play with Mrs. Henderson?"

Velly gaped at her. How could this tiny little child, with a brain the size of a lima bean, have managed to find her in an enormous crowd of people like this? It had to be almost impossible.

But no, thought Velly grimly as she closed her mouth again, it was not only possible, it was unavoidable. Velly was young, but she had already learned the Main Lesson Of Life — if you ever have something important to do, all by yourself, Abigail Braintree will certainly be there within twenty seconds.

"Abigail, what are you doing here? Go away!"

"Rumba likes SPREAD-O but Soapy doesn't. How come you did that to the SPREAD-O?" babbled Abigail. "We saw some big dolphins in the water last summer. Shiny. Did they like SPREAD-O? Did I tell you? Can I play with Mrs. Henderson, can I can I can I?"

"Not now, Abigail," said Velly.

"Pleeeeeeaaaaaasse????"

"No! I'm busy right now," said Velly, "but I'll tell you what — I think she's hungry. Why don't you go and get Mrs. Henderson something to eat, all right?"

"Like what, Velly?" said Abigail in a loud voice. "Like potato chips or lettuce? Like graham crackers Velly or avocoddles or caddoes or or onions in a jar or like little pumpkins or food coloring?"

"I don't know . . . anything! Just go and see, okay?"

"Like mustard? Like jelly beans? Mashed potatoes? Teabags? Pickle relish? Margarine? Soda crackers? Cherry popsicles? Little marshmallows shaped like —"

"Abigail, we're at the SPREAD-O peanut butter show," said Velly, trying to be patient, "so why don't you get her some *peanut butter*?"

"That's um . . ." said Abigail slowly, and then her face suddenly brightened. "That's a super good idea Velly!" she said, and crawled swiftly back out from under the podium and into the crowd.

"If we're lucky, she won't be back soon, Mrs. Henderson," she said, but in the pit of her stomach she knew they would have to be very lucky indeed. She was so nervous that her ears were sweating. She would have to pull off some very delicate feats in the next few minutes, all of which would require great skill and daring and expert timing, and that meant it was almost guaranteed that Abigail would be back at her side hopelessly quickly.

Oh well, nothing to do but to get started, thought Velly. She pulled the egg carefully from Mrs. Henderson's box and crept up beneath the Principal's chair.

Above her, the Mr. Box was muttering softly to himself, almost too quietly for Velly to hear what he was talking about. He was trying to work out what he would say when it was his turn to speak.

"Citizens of Snudsley, something like that," he mumbled as he paced back and forth, "I've solved the case. The Larp hooligans are this Parsley and this Sprout — and then I'll push them forward or something — and they are completely and scandalously guilty, and now you can throw anything you like at them, perhaps rotten tomatoes . . ."

He looked around quickly — not a police agent in sight. He wasn't having much luck. There weren't any other people in Snudsley apart from the police whom he could trust to get the girls and deliver them to the Presentation. Those girls were sneaky. They were tricky. There were bound to get away from anyone but a policeman.

"I suggest," he muttered on, "no, I *insist* that you, the good people of Snudsley, begin melting tar and collecting feathers — at once!"

He could imagine the cheers, and the wild applause. If only he could find a way to get those two horrible little girls over here . . .

"Yes, Mr. Whacker," the Mayor was saying, "this little Larp brouhaha has certainly created a bit of a stir, but I'm quite sure things will go more smoothly after today's Presentation."

"Well, I sincerely hope so," said Mr. Whacker. "We at SPREAD-O feel that everything will get back to normal once this glorious new factory is complete." He was looking nervous and ill at ease — but, as was previously pointed out, he always looked this way so it's impossible to say if he felt rotten or actually pretty well.

Suddenly he felt a clumsy, furry tap on his shoulder.

"Mr. Whacker, sir?" said a muffled voice.

"Trevellyn!" exclaimed Mr. Whacker.

Llewellyn Trevellyn looked quite different from his last appearance in this story — gone was the light blue fedora, the tailored silk suit, the walking stick and the pearl-gray gloves. In their place he wore a huge and somewhat thread-bare squirrel suit, covered with reddish-brown fur, and he watched Mr. Whacker through the large googly cartoon eyes of his false, bucktoothed head.

"Why are you up here?" demanded Mr. Whacker. "You should be out there, working the crowd!"

"I was *en route* for that very purpose, noble sir," came the muffled reply.

"What? I can't hear you with that stupid head on."

"Sorry about that," said Llewellyn, pulling off the huge foam head. "It was merely my intention to notify you of my imminent departure, sir."

"Well, I thought you'd already gone. Now get out there, spy on everyone, and bring me back something I can use to wipe out Tode and Nut-Tastic."

"Spy on," wondered Llewellyn, "everyone?"

"In a case like this," said Mr. Whacker, "absolutely *no one* is above suspicion. Somewhere out there in the crowd is a person or persons who mean to destroy SPREAD-O for good, so stop wasting time and get out there and find them. *Now!*"

"At your pleasure, sirrah," said Llewellyn, and he bowed, and climbed lumberingly down off the platform and into the crowd.

"Stupid actor," mumbled Mr. Whacker, but when he turned back to his conversation he was shocked to see that, instead of facing the Mayor, he was looking directly into the thin, smiling face of —

"Tode!" he gasped. "What are you doing here?"

"Ah, you two know each other, do you?" said the Mayor pleasantly from behind the Nut-Tastic president's shoulder. "Good. I'll leave you to chat a bit. I must go and see if the architects are ready with their materials."

"Wha — wha —?" sputtered Mr. Whacker, after the Mayor had gone. He was trying to retain his composure, but Mr. Tode was the last person he had expected to see today. What was the treacherous devil trying to prove?

"Well now. Tode," said Mr. Whacker at last. "Tode. Mr. Tode. How are Ratty and Mole?"

"Oh how funny," said Mr. Tode drily. "Oh my sides. I've never heard that one before, Weed, that's really quite witty of you."

"It's pronounced Wade," said Mr. Whacker tightly. "It's Swedish. My parents came from Sweden, and it's pronounced Wade."

"Your parents came from ten miles outside Cedar Rapids," said Mr. Tode, "and it's *Weed*."

"Look, Tode," hissed Mr. Whacker, growing redder in the face each moment, "you've got a lot of nerve coming here, after what you've done."

"What do you mean, 'what I've done'?" said Mr. Tode smoothly. "After doing some market research, Weed, we merely decided to change the name of the product, and —"

"*I know you did, you toad!*" screamed Mr. Whacker, lunging for Mr. Tode's throat.

As Velly crouched *underneath* the podium, and Mr. Whacker and Mr. Tode were battling it out on *top* of the podium, Rennie stood beside Ken and Lily's muffin table at the *side* of the podium, looking up at her parents onstage and wrestling with her own inner demons. What could she do to help everybody out of the mess she had created? She had no idea — she always had plenty of brilliant ideas, but never ideas about helping out other people. She didn't even know how to go about thinking of them.

While she was looking down at Ken's Veg-Spread and organic muffin display, she heard a familiar voice whispering into her ear.

"Perhaps you ought to take some of those Carrot Crumpets to your parents," said White Rennie. "That would show a good spirit."

"I can't see how that could help," said Rennie, "since they taste like old shoes that have been in a well."

"But they will know they are from Ken and Lily, and it will show your Good Intentions," said White Rennie. "You can say to your mom and dad, 'Ken and Lily are sorry about everything and want you to have these as a gift.'."

Well, that seemed like a pretty good idea, and Rennie wanted to help the two families to be friends again at least, even if she couldn't stop all the rest of the nonsense she had caused. She slathered four Carrot Crumpets with lots of gummy Eggplant Crème, put them on a plate, and began to pick her way through the crowd towards the podium, where Clive and Helen were still busy setting up for their Presentation.

"I'll take these to mom and dad," she told herself, "and it will be super nice, and we'll all be friends again." She was quite pleased with herself, but on the way to the podium she heard a different familiar voice in her other ear.

"Or you *could* say, 'Ken and Lily are sorry about everything and want you to have these *horrid, doughy lumps* as a gift!',," said Red Rennie. "Or, instead of saying any of that, why don't you just forget the whole thing and shove those sticky crumpets right under the Principal's tail when he sits down? It would be easy. His chair is pushed right up to the back of the podium."

"But that's not super nice . . ."

"It's *better* than super nice," said Red Rennie in a sooth-ing voice, "it's *funny*. Besides, you promised Velvet you would think up a plan to get revenge against the Principal. And so you're just keeping your promise. And so that's *ultra*-super nice, isn't it?"

Rennie looked at the crumpets for a moment.

"Hee hee," she said.

After Llewellyn Trevellyn had been dispatched by Mr. Whacker into the crowd, another unseen drama was unfold-ing deep within the recesses of the well-known squirrel suit.

The once-famous actor felt himself ready to take on the greatest role of his career — that of Squee, Super Secret Squirrel Spy.

"Hidden agents, hidden agents," he said to himself as he moved through the crowd, trying to give everyone within reach their free samples of SPREAD-O. "There may be hidden Nut-Tastic agents in the crowd. It is my task, nay my *duty*, to sniff them out, and by sniffing, discover them and expose their devilish intrigues."

There certainly were a bewildering amount of people milling around, and after a bit of careful observation, Llewellyn had to admit that he didn't know if he could recognize a hidden agent, in the unlikely event that he could actually see one through the little eyes cut out of the front of his Squee head.

"In theory," he mused, "people might look suspicious if they were on the point of robbing a bank, or kicking a puppy, or getting ready to throw a pie at someone. But how does one look suspicious if they are in the middle of an enormous peanut butter label-switching conspiracy? What would such a ruffian look like?"

For example — here on the pavement was an old man with a metal walker, there a young woman holding an ice cream cone. And there, beside the lamppost, a young couple indulged in an amorous encounter. A small child sat on a bench under a tree, playing with a fallen leaf. A stoutish bald man walked slowly, holding two Pomeranians on thin leashes. A tall, thin man with a beard and baseball cap picked his thumbnail lazily and waited for the speeches on the podium to begin. Any one of them, reflected Llewellyn, may have been the Larp culprit.

"Alas, I am all in despair," Llewellyn said desperately to himself. "These scoundrels are not easily detected."

"Howdy, there, tenderfoot! Free Larp?" said a voice to his left. He turned quickly around to face another large animal, almost the same size as himself, holding out a friendly paw, which contained a tiny jar of Larp.

"This *has* to be the Shane the Shrew," thought Llewellyn craftily. "Surely *he* must be a hidden agent. Who would know more about the Larp scandal than the evil Nut-Tastic mascot?"

"Howdy, tenderfoot. Free Larp," repeated Shane. "Do you want it or not, man?"

"Certainly, noble beast," said Llewellyn, taking the jar graciously, "but can it be that you know me not?"

"Nope," said Shane. "I can't see anything out of this head. But you sound like an English teacher I once had."

"I am — *Squee!*" said Llewellyn triumphantly.

"Oh," said Shane, and he moved on to the next person. "Howdy, there, tenderfoot. Free Larp?"

"No, listen. I'm Squee," said Llewellyn, following him. "You know, *Squee*. You simply must know me — Squee the Squirrel, from SPREAD-O? The Peanut Butter Lover's Forest Friend?"

"Look, I just started a week ago," said Shane. "I'm new. I only figured out how to work the tail this morning. I never heard of you."

"But I'm Squee," repeated Llewellyn.

"C'mon, leave me alone! I gotta hand out this Larp!"

"Well, *your* Larp is a pestilence, sir!" shrieked Llewellyn, and he shoved Shane roughly, spilling little Nut-Tastic Larp jars all over the street. "And you are an ill-bred hooligan!"

"Hey!" cried Shane, pushing back. "Don't push me around, man!"

A shoving match between a gigantic shrew and a gigantic squirrel in the middle of Main Street was not a common event in Snudsley, and it was certainly more interesting than watching the Mayor and Principal tapping microphones on the podium. Before long most of the people had dashed away from the stage and quite a little crowd had gathered around the two enormous animals.

"You show him what for, Squee!"

"Don't let him push you around, Shane!"

Llewellyn walked over to Shane and pushed him again as Shane was trying to pick up his scattered jars.

"I shall push whom I like, vandal!" he declared. "Especially Larp-loving little omnivores like you!"

"It's a good thing for you I don't understand words like that," said Shane heatedly, "or you'd be in big trouble!"

"Oh I would, would I?" exclaimed Llewellyn, and he gave Shane a tremendous push.

"That's the boy, Squee!"

At that point Shane lost his balance, spun sideways for a moment and then fell backwards into a young girl who was pushing her way towards the podium, carrying a plate of four dreadful looking crumpets spread with Eggplant Crème.

". . . the world would be so much nicer if, instead of having wars, everyone gave one another yummy muffins," White Rennie was saying, "and what's more, I think — OOOOOF!"

At the moment of impact she shot off of Rennie's shoulder like a rocket-propelled ping-pong ball and flew into the crowd. The crumpets flew directly upwards and Rennie fell

to her stomach onto the street.

"Whoa, sorry, kid," Shane told her, as he struggled to get to his feet, "but this rat is hassling me!"

"I'm a *squirrel*, you upstart!" screamed Llewellyn.

Shane pushed Llewellyn away and held out a paw to Rennie, who wasn't actually hurt, and they both got to their feet and began to collect up their muffins and Larp jars, just as an deep voice boomed out over the crowd.

"Ahem. Ahem," said the voice, which belonged to the Mayor. "Ladies and Gentlemen, the *Visions of Snudsley SPREAD-O Factory Presentation* is about to begin."

There was a smattering of polite applause at this, but in fact the Presentation wasn't quite ready to begin, since in the center of the podium, behind the Mayor's back, Mr. Whacker was trying very hard to throttle the life out of a purple-turning Mr. Tode. He was doing rather better than you might expect, for while Mr. Tode was younger and stronger than Mr. Whacker, Mr. Whacker had the advantage of surprise, since Mr. Tode hadn't the faintest idea what Mr. Whacker was talking about when he screamed —

"Admit it, you creep! You're trying to destroy SPREAD-O! You changed our labels!"

Finally Mr. Tode wrenched Mr. Whacker's hands from his neck.

"What? Changed *your* labels? What are you talking about?"

"Changed my peanut butter labels to Larp labels," wheezed Mr. Whacker.

Mr. Tode caught his breath. He looked genuinely puzzled.

"But," he stammered after a moment, "I thought you did that, Weed. I thought it was supposed to be a Terrific Marketing Campaign."

Then Mr. Whacker looked genuinely puzzled.

"It's Wade," he said. "But didn't I just hear you say, 'I merely decided to change the name of the product . . .'?"

"Yes, the product, *my* product," said Mr. Tode. "Nut-Tastic didn't want to be left off the bandwagon with this Larp thing, so we changed all *our* labels. We now make Nut-Tastic Larp and it's turning out brilliantly."

This was not what Mr. Whacker had expected from his greatest enemy and fiercest rival. He looked spectacularly confused and just stood there for a full minute, with his mouth hanging open like an old sock on a clothesline. Finally he managed to comb his disheveled hair with his fingers, straighten his tie, and whisper:

"But then — who — how did — why —?"

"I've no idea, old boy," grinned Tode, "but it's nothing to do with me."

"And so," continued the Mayor into the microphone, "without further ado, I would like to present Mr. Weed Whacker, the president of SPREAD-O and the guiding light behind the new factory project, which promises to bring so much distinction and honor and glory and money to the Snudsley area. Mr. Weed Whacker?"

As the people applauded politely, Mr. Whacker took the folder of papers from Miss Limb and shambled up to the microphone. He had rehearsed this speech many many times, but after what Mr. Tode had said, it was as if he had never seen it before.

So Tode wasn't behind the Larp-switch? Who else could it be? Another peanut butter company? Burton Gleaming at Pea-Licious? Doug MacMistie over at Cap'n P-Nutt? It couldn't be Old Man Clogg at Smeeeeeer, they had played golf together for years. Who was it then? Who who who?

All the statistics and promises and clever sayings swam before his eyes, and he suspected that part of his speech was written in a foreign language, because he couldn't understand some of the words. For someone who generally felt uncomfortable and ill-at-ease, this moment was probably the most uncomfortable and the ill-at-easiest he had ever experienced.

His speech meaningless gibberish, his mind a deluxe six-course buffet of confusion, he looked out over the sea of faces. Finally something occurred to him to say.

"Actually, it's pronounced Wade," he said.

"Vision of the future . . . boldly taking risks . . . thirty percent . . . ship of prosperity . . . nestling in the port of secure investment . . ."

And so on and so on. I won't bore you with the whole of Mr. Whacker's speech, after he finally recovered himself enough to deliver it — it wasn't that interesting and it isn't important to the story anyway. What was much more interesting than what was happening on stage were two things that would have happened whether Mr. Whacker had bothered to deliver his speech or not.

The first was that the fight between Squee and Shane was still going on in the crowd. Someone had managed to break them up during their previous skirmish, and they had both tried to resume their jobs — to circulate through the crowd handing out samples of their respective products. But every now and then their paths would cross, and then one of them would take a swipe at the other one. It had from time to time gotten uglier even than that, and once Squee actually tried to knock all of Shane's samples out of his bag, and then step on them. At another point Shane tried to remove Squee's head.

The other much more interesting thing was Velly's situation behind the podium. Thanks to the Squee and Shane dust-up, the police had all been far too busy to notice her, quacking hatbox and all, and so she and her egg had been patiently waiting right underneath and behind Mr. Box's chair. But unfortunately the Principal hadn't sat in down his chair once during the entire time she had been waiting there. In fact he had been pacing swiftly around the platform, looking quite anxious. When a policeman would pass by, the Principal would leap at him and start barking all sorts of demands.

"Listen, you've *got* to go and get these *two girls* from the Snudsley Primary School! I locked them up in there! It's *all right*, I'm the *Principal!* They're a danger to *you*, and to *me*, and

to *all of civilization!* Get a *squad car*, bring them here *quickly*,
and get some *rotten tomatoes* too, if you think of it!"

But all he got from any of the policemen was a funny
look. And so he would fume a bit and then start pacing
some more.

However, Velly wasn't particularly worried about Mr.
Box — she knew that he would sit down eventually, and
then at some point would rise and applaud, and then he
would sit back down. That would all happen soon enough,
she knew it. But it was taking far too much time.

And Velly knew that sitting in one place, not moving,
tensely waiting for something important to happen, for a
very long time, could only lead to one thing . . .

"Hi Velly, hi Mrs. Henderson," said Abigail, coming
up under the podium and dragging Rumba and Soapy with
her. "I got some SPREAD-O for Mrs. Henderson. I got

it from a great big rat. Why have you got that egg, is that egg from Mrs. Henderson? Could I have a Mrs. Henderson egg too?" And she reached for Mrs. Henderson's hatbox, but before she could grab it Velvet slapped her hand down hard on the lid.

"No Abigail," she whispered through gritted teeth. "You can't have a Mrs. Henderson egg. You can't have anything. You can sit there and *be quiet.*"

Suddenly, she heard Mr. Whacker say something over the loudspeaker that the crowd liked, and after all the people had stopped applauding, everyone began to sit down, including Principal Box.

This was it! Abigail was silent for once, staring with large eyes as Velly lifted Mrs. Henderson's precious egg up and onto the seat of the Principal's chair.

But that was strange, very strange. Velly wondered why would someone put a mirror next to the Principal's chair?

There must have been one, because just as she was reaching up to put the egg on Mr. Box's chair, she saw *another* hand reaching up, on the other side of the chair, also putting a small roundish thing on the Principal's chair.

But then, it couldn't really be a mirror, because the non-Velly hand wasn't holding a duck egg. In fact Velly recognized it as one her mother's famous Cosmic Carrot Crumpets, spread with Eggplant Crème.

"What the heck?" she said, and looked down under the chair's seat and between the legs. There she saw Rennie's face looking back at her.

"Rennie," she gulped. "What are you doing here? This is supposed to be *my* brilliant prank!"

"Oh, this isn't a prank," explained Rennie, "this is a extra-super-nice thing I'm doing to help everyone and make everything nice and all right again for us and our two families. It's Good Intentions is what it is."

"What in the world are you babbling about? Have you snapped your cap or something?"

"Well, it was — supposed to be — I mean I thought it was — er, super nice — um," mumbled Rennie, but she never got to explain further, because they both suddenly felt an irresistible urge to look up. They did, and you can probably guess whose big, red, bug-eyed, mustached face they saw looking down furiously at them.

"SPROUT! PARSLEY!" screamed Principal Box.

"THANK GOODNESS YOU'RE HERE! I MEAN HOW DARE YOU? WHAT ARE YOU DOING HERE? HOW DID YOU GET OUT OF THAT ROOM? I LOCKED YOU IN MYSELF!" [1]

Then he looked more closely at his chair, and saw the egg and the crumpet, and his eyes grew even huger and buggier, and his mustache wigglier and wigglier, and that's when he really lost his temper, I'm afraid.

"WHAT WHAT WHAT'S THIS?" [2] he cried.

"Um, er . . ." was all the girls could say.

"Get back to that room IMMEDIATELY and lock yourselves in!"

---

1. He really did sound as if he was talking all in capital letters like that.

2. And this time I wish I could show you how loud he was talking, but they won't let me use letters that big.

"Er . . ." they repeated.

"Get out of here! No, wait! Stay here! Get up on this podium! No, get out! No, wait!"

As they watched the Principal quivering back and forth like this, Rennie and Velly momentarily stopped paying close attention to Abigail. The little girl saw her chance, and she took it. With skillful, pudgy little hands she removed the wooden pin from the lid of Mrs. Henderson's box and opened it.

"QUAAAAAACK!"

Mrs. Henderson was so overjoyed at being out of the box, and at seeing Velly and Rennie, (but mostly Rennie), that she hopped and flapped and flopped with ecstasy all over the place, up and around the two girls, back and forth between them and Abigail, and into the Principal's face, honking and clacking and scraping, and you couldn't tell where she was from one second to the next.

"Quack Quack Quack Quack!"

"What on EARTH is THIS?" shrieked the Principal.

At that moment Mrs. Henderson must have been certain that this was the best day she had ever spent in her entire tiny life, because not only was she out of her hatbox, and together with all her favorite people, but she also saw lying under the chair and on its seat her heart's delight — four big crumpets smeared with loads and loads of her new favorite food, Ken Sprout's Eggplant Crème.

"QUAAAACK!"

She gobbled one crumpet down instantly and trod on another and flung the other two in different directions in her mad happiness. At least one got Mr. Box on the side of the face, and I think it actually may have been two.

Then Mrs. Henderson sprang in a joyful feathery arc, ten feet in the air and over the Principal's head. He threw his arms over his face and lost his balance, crashing backwards over his chair and collapsing onto the podium with feathers and Eggplant Crème all over his upper body.

"Let's um . . ." said Rennie.

"Go?"

"Yes."

And Rennie and Velly ran like rabbits into the crowd.

The Principal lay there on the wooden planks, looking up at the sky and trying to imagine what had just happened to him, and wondering why he hadn't stayed out of the education business altogether and taken his parents' advice to become a drill-press operator, when he heard a small voice next to his ear.

"Hi Mr. Mustache-Man, it's me Abigail Braintree. I'm four and three-quarters years old. You know what, Mr. Mustache-Man?"

A weary voice came from the mound of crumpet crumbs, smeared Eggplant Crème, rumpled suit and disheveled mustache.

"No, I don't. What's that, Abigail?"

"I know what they were doing, Rennie and Velly. Rennie and Velly were changing the SPREAD-O jars. That's what they were doing."

"Oh thank you, Abigail," said the Principal, "thank you so very much indeed."

"Can I have my twenty dollars now?"

Eight

Meanwhile, at the front of the podium, Mr. Whacker —
who seemed to be finding untapped resources of strength
within him — was continuing with his speech with more
and more gusto as he went on.

"My friends," he said in a round, full voice, "one promise
that I will always keep — no matter what has happened in
the past, and no matter what may happen in the future — I
promise that you will always be able to trust SPREAD-O
to bring you the finest *peanut butter* available to mankind,
the *peanut butter* you have always known, the *peanut butter*
you have always cherished and held close to —"

"Boooooo!" The crowd started to boo and hiss at the
words "peanut butter", and several began to chant "P.B. out,
Larp in!" over and over.

"No! No! Listen, my friends, you don't understand!"

"P.B. out, Larp in!"

People were shouting all around them, but after fighting their way through the crowd, Rennie and Velly found a fairly quiet spot behind a tree where they could talk.

"I'm confused," said Rennie. "Have you got any idea of what actually is going on right now?"

"I think those business types up there are fighting about *who* gets to call *what* 'Larp'," said Velly.

"What a big bunch of clucks," said Rennie. "I had no idea that so many people take peanut butter so seriously."

"Or that so many actual people make the stuff," said Velly. "I thought it was like bubblegum or chocolate bunnies. You know, made by elves or something."

"By the way," asked Rennie, "what were you going to do with that egg?"

"Oh, I was trying to be the Prank Queen and pull off a brilliant joke," sighed Velly. "But I'm not very good at it. What was with you and those crumpets?"

"Well, I was trying to be sensitive and super nice and I'm *terrible* at it," said Rennie with a smile. "And somehow I decided at the last second to put the crumpet on the Principal's chair. I still can't believe I came up with such a hopeless gag as that."

"I think we work much better together," said Velly. "Mr. Sticky, and the newspaper, and *Operation Larp* — well, they were elegant and clever."

"I agree," said Rennie, "and having the Principal sit on muffins and eggs was hardly up to our usual standards. I bet even Mrs. Henderson could have come up with better ideas than those."

"Oh my gosh, Mrs. Henderson!" exclaimed Velly. "I forgot all about her — she's still up there. But they'll be sure to catch us if we go up to the podium, won't they? I guess she'll be all right by herself for while."

"I'm not so sure," said Rennie. "If she's hanging around the podium, she might be in for some trouble. Just look at them — they've all gone crazy up there."

She was right — apart from the general chaos in the crowd, they could see Mr. Tode trying to grab the microphone from Mr. Whacker, the Mayor and the other dignitaries trying to shout things at each other, and a messy-looking Principal Box hopping up and down and yelling for the police.

"You are so right," said Velly. "Let's go get Mrs. Henderson."

"P.B. out, Larp in!"

Mr. Whacker's only hope to save his company had been to persuade the people how stupid Larp was and how sensible peanut butter was, but in his heart he now knew it was probably a losing battle. Until today he hadn't realized how popular Larp had become, even though it was still the exact same stuff in the exact same jar.

"Listen everyone," he said into the microphone, "please stop chanting for a moment and listen."

"P.B. out, Larp in! P.B. out, Larp in!"

"Now CUT THAT OUT! Listen, friends, you don't want 'Larp', whatever it is, you want 'peanut butter', just as you always have, SPREAD-O peanut butter. Come to your senses, please! I — what is this *duck* doing here? No really, listen. Peanut butter is sensible. It means something. 'Larp' isn't even a real word. 'Larp' doesn't mean anything!"

Down in the crowd, Velly turned to Rennie.

"Did you hear that?"

"He said 'duck'," said Rennie.

"Let's go," said Velly, and they began to push themselves through the people towards the podium, where Mr.

Tode had seized the microphone from Mr. Whacker.

"Larp? Means nothing?" he cried. "Ladies and gentlemen, I do not think so. No, not at all. What does Larp mean to you? Freedom, that's what! The tyranny of the past — overthrown! The mindless acceptance of peanut butter — demolished! No more will we have to eat something that's called butter when it isn't. What does Larp mean? I'll tell you — it means something bright, something shining. Larp means a promise — it means *tomorrow*. Larp means *something new!*"

This speech brought a tremendous cheer from the crowd, and Mr. Tode's smile beamed out over all the people, and for once it seemed like a genuinely happy smile. He had won the day.

Several people had hoisted Shane up on their shoulders and bore him, like a Roman emperor, through the crowd and set him on the stage next to Mr. Tode. Mr. Tode put his arm around the shrew's fuzzy shoulders and they both waved happily at the ecstatic crowd.

Mr. Whacker, by contrast, looked like someone who had just received some very bad news from the tax board. His skin was sort of green, and he appeared so small and crumpled you might think he was made entirely of old wads of damp paper. Miss Limb came over to him and patted him on the back.

"Oh Mr. Whacker," she said sympathetically, "is there anything I can do?"

"Yes, Miss Limb," said Mr. Whacker in a soft, strangled voice, "you can probably start looking for a new job. We've lost. SPREAD-O is finished."

He slunk down, unnoticed by the other people on the podium, and vanished into the crowd like a wisp of sorry smoke.

The Parsleys were also looking pretty miserable. Their little model stood proudly in its glass box, just as lovely and clean as though it would actually be built someday, but it looked now as if that day would never come. If SPREAD-O was finished, that little model was the last thing *Parsley & Parsley, Architects* would ever build.

Slowly they gathered their plans and charts together and started to put their drawings and diagrams back into their folders.

"Oh well, Helen," said Clive in a thick voice, "I guess it's back to the —"

"Don't say it," gulped Helen. "I can't bear to hear it."

"No, I was going to say 'the painting-and-decorating business'," sighed Clive. "I'm afraid that this is the end of *Parsley & Parsley*."

Just then the Principal staggered by and pointed his smudgey finger at Clive.

"PARSLEY!" he cried.

"What is it, Mr. Box?" said Clive.

"Your daughter, Parsley, where is she?" demanded the Principal.

"I don't know. Why?"

"Do you see all this?" said Mr. Box, sweeping his arm out over the crowd. "Do you know who's responsible? Your daughter, that's who! Her and that Sprout girl. The police are keeping it quiet, but I'm on my way to proclaim the TRUTH to the world!"

"Rennie and Velly?" asked Helen. "But how could they be responsible for this mess?"

"Larp! That's how!" screamed the Principal. "I don't know what they did, or how they did it, but they were caught red-handed doing it, whatever it was. And I warn you, if I get my hands on them again, I'll —"

We will sadly never know what the Principal would have done if he ever got his hands on Rennie and Velly again, since his voice was cut short suddenly — and this was because he had been knocked off his feet and over to the opposite side of the stage by an enraged squirrel, who appeared out of nowhere at that moment and began racing like a lunatic towards Shane the Shrew, who was still standing at the front of the podium with Mr. Tode and waving to the crowd.

"Larp for everyone!" cried Mr. Tode.

"No more peanut butter!" shouted Shane.

"Vengeance is mine!" squealed Llewellyn, and he tackled Shane from behind and knocked him off his feet. Then he leapt on him and made for his throat. Shane tried kicking Squee off of him, but this proved too difficult, because the Shane suit was big and bulky; designed more to move slowly through a crowd distributing samples of Larp, and not for hand to hand combat with giant, angry squirrels.

"Dude I can't move. Get off!"

"Never!"

"Cut it out!"

"I shall never weaken!"

But he did. After rolling around for ten minutes Llewellyn, too, found his strength fading away, and although both men in animal costumes gave it a courageous effort, the two of them soon collapsed into a state of total exhaustion.

At that moment it was as if all the steam had gone out of the town of Snudsley. The noisy chaos gave way to an eerie stillness that hung over the square, and everyone present seemed either exhausted or actually unconscious.

On one corner of the podium sat Abigail, feeding Mrs. Henderson with pieces of Carrot Crumpet. The duck was sitting happily and lazily in her hatbox — apparently she had been worn out by all the excitement. She barely quacked when Rennie picked her up and put her under her arm.

"Thanks, Abigail," she said.

"Yes," said Velly, "thanks for taking care of Mrs. Henderson."

"You're welcome," said Abigail.

The four of them — Rennie, Velly, Mrs. Henderson and Abigail — carefully made their way between the puddles of Veg-Spread, the demolished chairs and benches, broken jars of peanut butter and Larp, past the motionless bodies of various unconscious shrews, squirrels, Mayors and Principals, and towards the microphone. The crowd looked up at them, expectant but sort of drowsy, like a flock of sleepy sheep. It was Velly's small voice that finally broke the silence.

"Um, hello everyone," she said. "I just want to say — really, we didn't mean it."

"Yes, it was all just a kind of joke," said Rennie, "ha ha. Ha."

"We certainly didn't intend all of this," said Velly, "you know, we just switched some peanut butter labels."

"It was only twenty to start with," added Rennie.

"That's right, just twenty," said Velly.

"Now we want to say we're sorry," said Rennie, "and I think we should all just go home and try to forget all about everything, don't you?"

Nobody said a word.

"Yes, that would be best," agreed Velly, "even though we're sorry, just very sorry, just sorry, so sorry —"

"WOW! WOW WOWSY WOW WOW!"

"Terribly terribly —" continued Velly. "Hey, what was that?"

"I don't know," said Rennie. "I think it came from your mom and dad's muffin stand."

They both hopped off the stage and ran over to Ken and Lily's muffin table, where they were astonished to find Mr. Whacker, his face in a broad grin, and his hand clutching a Cosmic Carrot Crumpet slathered in Eggplant Crème.

"Mother of otters!" he cried. "This is terrific! It's exceptional! Mr. Sprout, you're a genius!"

"That's news to me," said Ken happily. "Usually my

stuff just makes everyone sick."

"Sick? How is it possible? This is a wonderful new taste sensation — it's so new it's new. It's newer even than Larp!"

There was applause from the crowd at this, and Rennie and Velly could hear people murmuring things like "I never thought it was that bad" and "Actually I prefer the Eggplant Crème to the Cabbage Whip".

Under Rennie's arm, Mrs. Henderson smelled the jar of Eggplant Crème nearby, and began to flap and quack wildly. Finally she squirmed away, and flew off into the crowd, with Abigail in pursuit.

Mr. Whacker seemed a changed man. No longer a tragic little puff of mist, he actually leapt up onto Ken and Lily's table like Robin Hood, and called boldly for the attention of the crowd.

"I want to announce to you, today, good citizens of Snudsley, that the SPREAD-O Company is *not* finished, and from now on we will dedicate ourselves to the production of this lovely lovely lovely new thing — Sprout's Eggplant Crème!"

There rose a great cheer from the crowd, and Mr. Whacker smiled and waved.

"Wait a minute," said Ken. He was standing next to Mr. Whacker, but he was on the ground and Mr. Whacker was standing on the table, so Ken had to pull the cuff of the ex-peanut butter president's trousers several times to get his attention.

"WAIT A MINUTE," he said again, more loudly this time.

"What is it, my good man?" said Mr. Whacker pleasantly.

"You can't make my Eggplant Crème if you're going to make it in a big noisy smelly factory," said Ken firmly. "I mean that's what we're here protesting against, after all!"

Mr. Whacker looked thoughtful for a moment.

"What if we changed the factory's design?" he asked at last. "Suppose we made a new one? A new plan for a brand new, up-to-the-minute, organic, non-polluting, zero-carbon factory right here in Snudsley — and not a factory either, but like a farm, or a windmill or something. And I'll even throw in your stupid crazy duck as our new mascot. Would that be all right?"

"Well sure!" said Ken and Lily together, and thinking of the money but also of moving out of the Parsley's house, they nodded vigorously.

Mr. Whacker then looked down from the table at Abigail, who was standing on the grass with Mrs. Henderson.

"And what's your ducky's name, little girl?"

Abigail, because she was a bit scared of him I suppose,
answered even more quickly and senselessly than usual —
which you know, if you have read this far, was very quickly
and senselessly indeed.

"Hi Mr. Man you're up on the table how come you're
up on the table we saw dolphins but they weren't on a table
last summer this is Soapy and this is Rumba sometimes
Soapy goes on the table but Rumba doesn't go on the table
because she falls off the table if I get twenty dollars I can

buy her some legs so she can stand on the table like you Mr. Man how come you're up —"

Rennie placed her hand quickly over Abigail's mouth so that only *mpf mpf* sounds came out.

"It's Mrs. Henderson," said Velly hastily, "the duck's name is Mrs. Elizabeth Henderson, sir."

"Mrs. Henderson," said Mr. Whacker doubtfully. "'Mrs. Elizabeth Henderson, the SPREAD-O Eggplant Crème Duck'. Oh well . . ."

He straightened up again and re-addressed the crowd.

"And I hereby charge," he declared, "that the firm of *Parsley & Parsley* should design a new SPREAD-O organic factory slash farm slash windmill thing here in Snudsley, where this new product will be manufactured in the most organic and healthiest and least smelly way possible. Oh heck, why stop there? We'll build a whole *network* of organic farm slash windmills, from California to Maine! Does that meet with the approval of the architects?"

Clive and Helen, who were thinking of the money but also of the Sprouts moving out of their house, nodded vigorously.

"And Nut-Tastic," said Mr. Tode suddenly over the loudspeaker, "will continue to provide the people of Snudsley with Larp, the fine quality Larp you have always loved so well for the past ten weeks or so!"

Well, that was the cue for more even cheering, and Rennie and Velly gave a huge sigh of relief.

"That was a close one," said Rennie.

"Thank heaven it all worked out," said Velly.

"It almost did," said a deep voice behind them, and they felt two large hands clap them on the shoulders. It was the police chief, of course, along with Principal Box.

The Principal looked even worse after being knocked over by Squee — he had a black eye and his hair was standing straight up, and he was covered with egg yolk and Eggplant Crème and feathers, but he had recovered consciousness and was grinning widely. He had finally arrived at his big shining moment.

"Ladies and gentlemen!" he announced in a loud voice. "I want everyone to know that these two girls, this so-called Sprout and Parsley, are COMPLETELY and HORRIBLY responsible for EVERY SINGLE ONE of

the mysterious Larp crimes!"

He smiled and looked around excitedly, but no one seemed to be as astonished as he had expected them to be.

"Didn't you hear me?" he asked. "It's them! They did it! They are guilty! Sprout and Parsley! Completely and utterly and filthily guilty!"

"You know," said Rennie quietly, "I think that everybody knew that already, Mr. Box."

"Oh well, in any case, it's two for the clink," said the chief of police, beginning to drag them off.

"Wait a moment, chief," said Mr. Whacker, climbing down off the table, "I don't want to press charges against these two. Sure, they're completely unhinged, and irritating, and responsible for all the chaos that's happened. I'll admit that. But still, this whole episode has given me the best business opportunity I ever had!"

Rennie and Velly tried to look extremely innocent.

"Besides," he went on, "they aren't really responsible for *all* of this, all they did was change a few labels."

"Well . . ." said the chief thoughtfully, "that's all right for you, Mr. Whacker, but what about Mr. Tode? He's involved as well, isn't he?"

"Oh, I'm sure Todey doesn't want to press charges," said Mr. Whacker eagerly. He looked up at Mr. Tode on the podium and shouted —

"Todey, do you want to press charges against these girls?"

"Don't call me 'Todey,' Weed," said Mr. Tode. "And of course I don't want to press charges. Those girls are marketing geniuses! I should press charges? I should give them a cash reward and a gold medal! I'm the new Larp King!"

"Hmmm. Well, if no one's pressing charges," said the police chief, releasing his hold on Rennie and Velly, "I can't hold you for anything. Sorry, Mr. Box."

The Principal was crestfallen again. His mustache twitched slightly and his eyes filled with tears. But after a moment he tugged at his lapels, and straightened his back, and addressed them in a very Principally tone.

"Very well," he said curtly, "can't have everything. You two get one more chance. But I promise you, I'm watching every move you make from now on. One more mistake, one teensy prank, even if it's just putting one grain of salt in the sugar shakers in the school cafeteria, anything at all — and it's the boiling lead. Boiling lead or the rack, one of the two. That's a promise."

He brushed a few stray duck feathers from his lapel and limped slowly away, wondering if by any chance they needed any primary school principals in Peru or Outer Mongolia . . .

Nine

Rennie gave Velly a big hug, and Velly hugged back.

"I guess that means you will be moving out of the house," said Rennie.

"Yep," said Velly. "Those nice people from Des Plaines can move nicely back to Illinois, and we Sprouts can move back into Grout Lane."

"I'll miss living with you," said Rennie. "It was fun."

"You can visit anytime, just as usual," said Velly. "Besides, it may have been fun for us, but our parents were having fits every five seconds."

"You're right," sighed Rennie. "And I've learned my lesson. No more pranks!"

Velly gave Rennie a *Oh Please Spare Me* look.

"Okay, well, how about no more pranks with eggs in

them?" asked Rennie. "The egg ones don't seem to work out very well."

"Good idea," said Velly. "It was chaotic with Mrs. Henderson's eggs today, and of course Mrs. Henderson started as an egg, let's face it. That duck's been nothing but trouble."

"No she hasn't!" protested Rennie. She opened the hatbox and peeped in. A soft quack came from inside, and Mrs. Henderson looked up at her with sleepy eyes.

"She looks satisfied," said Rennie, "she ate about five gallons of that Eggplant Crème. But she hasn't actually been a load of trouble, if you think of it. Neither of us managed to pull a prank on the Principal, but she did. She saved the day. When you guys move out I'm going to miss her."

Mrs. Henderson gurgled up at her with love.

"Now surely you don't think," said Velly, "that I would separate a youthful, happy, successful duck from her beloved mother? Never!" And she handed Rennie the hatbox.

"But," said Rennie, "but but but —"

"But me no but but buts," said Velly, "she loves you, and you'll be a fine mother. I'll be happy to help you out, but you won't need it. You can always go to the library and borrow a big duck book."

"Now, Sprout," Mr. Whacker was saying, "I want you to be in my office on Monday morning, so that we can start working on mass-production. And of course to discuss your position and salary."

"I'll be there," said Ken, giving Lily a gigantic hug. "Think of it, Lils — a Big Idea of mine finally paid off! 'Sprout's Eggplant Crème' in every shop, on every restaurant table, and sweeping the entire country with its wonderful goodness!"

"Isn't it exciting?" said Lily.

"The only problem I can see," mused Mr. Whacker, "is the name. 'Sprout's Eggplant Crème from SPREAD-O'. It doesn't have any *oomph*, it doesn't have any *zing*. Now, if only the stuff had a zippy new name . . ."

Everyone turned to look at Rennie and Velly, and Rennie looked at Velly, and Velly looked at Rennie.

And then they both began to smile . . .

TRACY WEIMAN

is an American author who lives in
Amsterdam with her friend Reine and
two cats, Satsuki and Mei.

ÁINE McWRYAT

is an Irish artist who lives on the island
of Eigg and keeps a breeding pair of gan-
nets; but she hasn't thought of their
names yet.

CPSIA information can be obtained
at www.ICGtesting.com
Printed in the USA
LVOW03s1015201217
560367LV00003B/423/P